CLARITY OF LINES

THE THOMAS ELKIN SERIES : BOOK TWO

N.R. WALKER

COPYRIGHT

Cover Artist: Reese Dante
Editor: Labyrinth Bound Edits
Thomas Elkin Series © 2017 N.R. Walker
Publisher: BlueHeart Press

Third Edition

December 2017

BLURB

Book two in the Thomas Elkin series

When some lines blur, others become crystal clear.

———

Absolutely smitten, Thomas Elkin and Cooper Jones have decided they're prepared to give a relationship a try.

What they're not prepared for is the reaction from their families, who try to force them apart.

Both men are about to learn that there are lines that define us. Sometimes the lines blur, sometimes the lines become crystal clear.

DEDICATION

For my husband...

THE
THOMAS ELKIN
SERIES

CLARITY
OF LINES
N.R. WALKER

CHAPTER ONE

THE VIEW from my office was spectacular. It was a beautiful, clear day. The sky was a brilliant blue and while most people would have cursed having to work; I was still smiling. Line five on my desk phone lit up. My personal line. I picked up the receiver knowing who it would be.

A familiar voice spoke in my ear. "Mr. Elkin."

I chuckled into the phone. "Mr. Jones." It was the third phone call that day. "Don't you have enough to do?"

"Oh, I have plenty," Cooper answered. "But you haven't agreed yet."

"I told you it wasn't really my scene. Why don't you take one of your other friends?"

"You mean *younger* friends. I don't want any of them to come with me. I want *you* to come with me."

Cooper had two tickets to see some god-awful, too-loud band at Madison Square Garden, and right or wrong, he wanted me to go with him.

"Is this not something we could discuss over dinner?"

"I like annoying you at work," he said cheerfully. "Usually if I pester you enough, you'll just agree with me to shut me up."

I groaned. "Is that a skill you work on, or is it a natural-born talent?"

"It's a Gen-Y thing."

"It's a Cooper-Jones thing."

He chuckled into the phone. Then his tone of voice changed to a playful whisper. "Come on, baby. You know you want to. It's Linkin Park. They're my favorite."

"Lincoln who?"

He burst out laughing this time, and I sighed. "I'll talk to you about it tonight," I told him. "Will you come over?"

"That depends." I could tell he was still smiling.

"On what?"

"On you saying yes to the concert."

"I have a lot to do today..."

"Then agree with me."

"Goodbye, Cooper."

I hung up, still smiling, and not even half a minute later, my private line lit up again. I pressed the flashing button and laughed. "All right, I'll go with you if it will shut you up so I can get some work done."

But Cooper didn't laugh. There was only silence. I quickly checked the line to confirm it was on my personal line and not a business call, just as another familiar voice said, "Excuse me?"

Shit.

Sofia. My ex-wife. I cleared my throat and said, "I thought you were someone else."

"Obviously."

I could have reminded her that *she* had called *me* on my private line at work, but instead I took a breath and started again. "Sofia, what can I do for you? Is everything okay?"

"Everything's fine," she said in a cool tone, like I had no right to ask. "I was just calling to remind you that Ryan's birthday is in three weeks."

"I remembered."

"Yes, well, he's thinking of having a party up at the Casa. I told him he needs to let me know by Friday so I can get it organized."

"Okay."

Then, not being one for small talk, she said, "He tells me you're seeing someone."

"Yes, I am," I said slowly, wondering—dreading—what Ryan had told her. "What else did Ryan say?"

"Nothing really," she said. "Just that you were getting serious."

I exhaled in relief. "Yes, well..." I wasn't sure what to say. I wasn't embarrassed or ashamed of Cooper in any way... it was just that I wasn't about to explain to my ex-wife over the phone that I was dating a man the same age as our son.

"Mmm," she hummed. I could picture the look of disdain on her face. "Well, whatever Ryan decides to do for his birthday, be sure to bring... your friend."

My friend.

Sure, she was ready to admit I was gay, but she wasn't ready to say 'him,' or 'he,' or 'boyfriend.'

The line clicked in my ear. Sofia also wasn't ready for amicable goodbyes.

Given I'd already just made one faux pas on the phone by assuming it was Cooper and been blindsided by my still-mad ex-wife, I decided text would be safer. At least I could see who the incoming messages were from.

I pulled out my cell and selected Cooper's cell number and typed out a message.

You're in so much trouble. Just took a call. Thought it was you. It wasn't.

My phone beeped a short time later. *LOL. Did you answer the phone with the offer of a BJ?*

I snorted. *Close.*

His reply was almost immediate. *LMAO.*

LMAO? Dear God. I really was dating a twenty-two year old. I typed, *Keep the first weekend of next month free.*

Okay.

He didn't even ask why. Then another message, *Keep the fifteenth of next month free. I bought TWO concert tickets.*

Did you ever take my NO seriously?

Nope. Now, about that BJ...

I smiled as I threw my phone into my top drawer. He was so horny. He wanted sex, he thought about sex, all the time. Not that I was complaining. I'd never been more satisfied, and I'd never been in better shape.

I needed to be fit just to keep up with him.

———

WHEN COOPER ARRIVED at my apartment, letting himself in with his own key, it was getting late. The sun was setting over the city, casting its final rays across my living room. I was in the kitchen reading through my mail. He walked in and kissed the side of my head. "Good evening, Mr. Elkin."

"Mr. Jones."

"You didn't reply to my text messages?"

When I had checked my phone before leaving, there were three messages from him, all wanting details on this supposed blow job I'd almost offered whoever had called my office.

"No, I didn't reply," I said, taking his hand and leading him to the sofa. I pushed him down so he was seated and I slowly knelt between his legs.

Cooper's eyes widened, as did his smile. "Well, I think I like this better."

Without taking my eyes off his, I undid his belt buckle, then the button on his pants, and I gently pulled down his fly. I slid the elastic of his briefs down to reveal my prize and ran my tongue over the head of his cock.

"Oh, fuck," he whispered. He spread his legs wider and lifted his hips, giving me more access. I licked him again and took him into my mouth, swirling my tongue and sucking him. He was hard in no time, making a whimpering noise.

He always made the sweetest sounds.

His fingers were in my hair and I could tell he was trying not to thrust into my mouth. He wanted more. So I took him deeper, deeper, opening my throat to take him down. Cooper arched his back and moaned, and I knew he was close. I cupped his balls with one hand and pumped the base of his cock with the other while I sucked the head, making him cry out. His cock swelled in my mouth, he gripped my hair, and he spurted hot and thick into my throat.

There wasn't anything like it.

It was empowering to make him come so quick and hard.

He let go of my hair, slumped into his seat, and groaned out a laugh. "Tom, Tom, Tom..."

I smiled rather proudly and got up off my knees, only to kneel over his thighs. Cooper's head lolled heavy on the back of the sofa. I put my hands on either side of his face and waited for him to lazily open his eyes. He grinned and put his hands on my hips, so I planted my mouth on his, letting him taste himself.

Cooper pulled my thigh down and pushed me sideways, back on the sofa, and lay over me, pressing down on me. He kissed me again, slower this time. "Well, that was better than a text message," he said with a smile.

"Much better," I agreed.

He opened the first two buttons on my shirt and kissed down my neck. "We should text each other more often."

I laughed and ran my hand down his back and over the curve of his ass, pushing his hips into mine. "Having messages from you about blow jobs was too distracting."

I could feel him smile against my neck.

"Mmm, I like making you think about sucking my dick. It makes turning up here a lot more fun."

I chuckled again and playfully bit his neck. "I've been thinking about doing that all afternoon."

Cooper pulled back and pecked my lips, twice. "So what am I doing the first weekend of next month that I would need to make sure I'm free for? Taking me away somewhere for a dirty weekend?"

"Not really. Sorry to disappoint. It's Ryan's birthday."

"Cool," he said, resting his head on his hand, his arm bent at the elbow. "That's not disappointing. It'll be fun. What are we doing?"

"We're heading up to the Hamptons."

His eyes widened, excited. "Really?"

"Don't get too excited," I warned him. "Sofia will be there. She wants to meet you."

His smile faded. "Sofia? Your ex-wife?"

I nodded. "Ryan's mother."

"She knows you're dating me?"

"No," I admitted. "But she's about to find out."

CHAPTER TWO

COOPER TOOK the prospect of meeting my ex-wife quite well. True to Cooper's form, he was inquisitive and asked a lot of questions. "Does she know *anything* about me?"

"She knows I'm seeing someone. She doesn't know who it is."

"How will she take it?"

"I don't know. I'd guess not well."

"Do you care what she thinks?"

"Not about me. Only when it concerns Ryan."

"And she called you?"

"Yes."

"Do you talk to her often?"

"No."

"Do you miss her?"

That question stopped me. "I used to. When we first separated," I told him. "I missed my friend. We were married for almost twenty years. It wasn't easy, particularly for her." I looked at him and smiled sadly. "But I don't miss her anymore."

"Tell me about it," he said softly. "Tell me what happened."

"Why I left her?"

He nodded. "I know *why* you left. Tell me what made you decide to do it."

I got up from the sofa, walked to the kitchen, and grabbed a bottle of merlot and two glasses, then walked back to the sofa. I poured us both a glass and left the bottle on the coffee table. Cooper waited, watching me patiently, and he smiled at me when I handed him the glass of red.

"I met Sofia in college. She was a driven woman, but a lot of fun. I was... curious... with guys. I knew I was attracted to them. I had a few... experiences, but I hung out with Sofia so people wouldn't suspect I was gay. I wasn't gay... well, that's what I told myself."

I sipped my wine, and Cooper curled his legs up underneath him and put his hand on my thigh, giving me his undivided attention.

I took a deep breath then continued, "My father would never have understood. He paid for my college tuition and kept a very close eye on me. He pushed me hard, and I wanted to make him happy."

"You married Sofia to make your father happy?" Cooper asked. There was no judgment in his eyes, just curiosity.

"It was expected of me," I said. "My parents knew Sofia's parents, and it was just assumed we'd be together. It was a different time then. It's just what you did. You went to college, got married, bought a house, had a family."

Cooper sipped his wine. "Did Sofia ever suspect you liked guys?"

I shook my head. "No. I thought it was an exploring thing. You know, in college you explore, experiment. In my twenties, I thought the attraction to men was just a phase that would pass. But it didn't. I struggled with it. I ignored it. I told myself I was happy with Sofia and that I should be grateful."

Cooper squeezed my thigh.

"But it got harder to ignore."

"Did you ever..." He hesitated. "You know, with a guy while you were married?"

"No," I said adamantly. "Never. I never cheated on Sofia. In my head, yes, a thousand times over I fantasized and dreamt about it..." I sighed. "I don't know, maybe that's just as bad."

"No, it's not," he answered quickly. "It's not, Tom. It's nothing like it. Fantasizing about it and actually doing it are two very different things."

I smiled at how he tried to placate me, and I sipped my wine. "And then I hit my thirties. I knew I had to do something. I knew I couldn't keep living a lie. But Ryan was in high school, and I didn't want to derail him. It wasn't a simple divorce," I said softly. "I didn't just have to tell him I was moving out and that his mom and I were separating. I had to tell him *why*."

Cooper refilled our glasses and patiently waited for me to speak again.

"It was my thirty-ninth birthday, and I just knew. I knew I had to come clean. I felt if I got to forty and was still living a lie, then it was all over. I don't know why, it's just how I felt. I'd waited and waited so long, then all of a sudden I couldn't wait anymore. I felt like I was drowning..."

Cooper moved closer to me and slid his hand into mine. "Oh, Tom."

"I told Sofia the truth, and while it felt like a weight was off my chest, I simply transferred the weight to her. She was devastated."

"I'm sure she'll understand," Cooper said with a nod. "In time."

"It's been five years. She's still very angry with me and I don't blame her," I admitted. "I hurt her very deeply. She was the one who had to face all her friends and associates and tell them her husband was gay."

"But you didn't have a choice," Cooper replied simply. "You couldn't have denied yourself happiness forever."

"My happiness or hers?" I asked rhetorically. "And I *did* have a choice. I shouldn't have married her, I should have told her twenty years before, when we were kids in college. But we have Ryan, and he means the world to me. But I still should have told her."

"You couldn't," he countered. "Your father would have disowned you."

"He still would."

Cooper was surprised by this. "Doesn't he know?"

"Well, my parents know I'm divorced, of course, much to their disgust. But not the reason why."

"Sofia never told them?"

I shook my head. "She's mad at me, yes, but she always loved my parents. She'd never hurt them."

"And Ryan?"

"He was very upset and embarrassed when I told him. It took a while, but he's okay with it now."

"He looks up to you." Cooper took another sip of wine. "It's not hard to see why. You're successful, brilliant, sexy as hell."

"I'm pretty sure that's not how Ryan sees me."

Cooper smiled. "So the Hamptons, huh? You never told me you had a place up there."

"I don't." I finished my wine. "Sofia does. I used to, but she got the apartment here in the City and the house in the Hamptons in the divorce settlement."

"What did you get?" he asked.

"I got my new gay life," I said with a smile. "Oh, and I bought this apartment."

Cooper shook his head, downing the rest of his drink. "I don't even want to know how much money you have. This apartment alone must have cost... You know what? Never mind."

I chuckled at him. "It was expensive, yes. But worth it, wouldn't you agree?"

He looked around the large room. "Um, yes, I would, very much. And then there's me," he said, putting his glass on the coffee table. "With nothing."

"You don't have nothing."

"No, you're right," he agreed. "I have a small *rented* apartment and a crushing college loan."

I lifted his hand to my lips and kissed his knuckles. "You have more than that." I didn't have to say anymore. I didn't have to tell him he had me. By the way he kissed me, I was pretty sure he knew.

———

"WHAT ARE YOU THINKING ABOUT?" Cooper rolled over and snuggled into my side. It was early morning and I'd been awake for a while, staring at the ceiling, thinking.

I was thinking about what to get Ryan for his birthday, but I was also thinking about what Sofia's reaction would be to meeting Cooper. "I need to know what to get Ryan for his birthday," I told him a half-truth.

"So you keep saying," he said.

"Well, you're his age, what should I get him?"

Cooper laughed into my chest then tweaked my nipple. "It's a gift from you. You need to pick it."

"Ooh, I know!" I said brightly. "You could give him the second ticket to that concert, and you could take him."

"Ha ha, very funny," he said, nipping my ribs. "Suck it up, old man. You're going with me whether you like it or not."

I rolled him onto his back and settled myself on top of him. His morning wood was pressed hard between us and I rocked back and forth. "Oh, that's a shame. I would *suck it* up all right, but I have an early meeting this morning."

Cooper bit his bottom lip and grinned, pushing his hips up against mine. "If you suck my dick, I'll tell you what Ryan told me he wanted for his birthday."

I tried to act like I was offended by his blatant blackmail, but he knew damn well I'd do it. So I took him to the edge of orgasm again and again, making him beg me, literally beg me, to finish him.

When I left for work, he was still a quivering, convulsing mess, barely coherent. But I made the meeting on time and had Jennifer make some phone calls to find out what the hell an Xbox 3D was.

CHAPTER THREE

THREE WEEKS later on the Friday afternoon after work, I put the suitcases and Ryan's present into the trunk of my Mercedes R171 while Cooper got into the passenger seat. He loved my car. I didn't drive it often—with a company car and driver for all work trips, I had no need to—but outside work when we did go somewhere, he loved it.

He was oddly excited about this trip, while I was almost dreading it.

"Did you really get the new Xbox?" he asked excitedly. "From Japan? It hasn't been released here yet!"

"Yes," I told him. "It cost me a fortune."

Cooper clapped his hands and kind of wiggled in his seat. "I cannot wait."

"Did *he* want it, or *you*?" I asked, pulling the car out onto the street. "Because you said *he* wanted it."

"Oh, he does," he said brightly. "I just share his enthusiasm."

I couldn't help but chuckle at him. "Remind me again why my boyfriend is twenty-two?"

"Because I was born twenty-two years after you, my

dear forty-four-year-old boyfriend," he said cheerfully. "And because I'm amazing."

I rolled my eyes sarcastically. "Oh, that's right. Now I remember."

"Is your Alzheimer's kicking in?" he asked with a laugh. "Should I drive, old man?"

"You're a little shit," I mumbled. "And don't blame it on Gen Y. It's all you."

He grinned, seemingly pleased with himself. "Oh, my favorite doorman, Lionel, said to have a good weekend."

"Were you giving him a hard time again?"

"Of course not."

Which meant of course, yes. "What did you say to him this time?"

He chuckled. "I told him your neighbor, old Mrs. Giordano, might like to have your apartment exorcised while you're out. Apparently she hears a man moaning at nighttime, for hours at a time. I told him I hear it too, but it's really nothing for her to be concerned about."

I stared at him. "You didn't."

He grinned proudly. *Shit. He really did.*

"Leave Lionel alone," I said. "The poor guy."

"He loves me."

"I thought he hated you."

"It's impossible to resist my charms."

"Yes," I said with a laugh. "I know."

As I maneuvered through New York traffic, Cooper rifled through the backpack at his feet and pulled out an iPod. He grinned at me. The kind of grin that made me worry. "What?"

"How long does it take to drive to the Hamptons?"

"Just over an hour and a half," I answered. "Why?"

"Long enough for you to become intimately acquainted with Linkin Park."

I groaned and he laughed.

"You'll need to know some songs before the concert."

"Resistance is futile, isn't it?" I deadpanned.

He connected his iPod through the car's Bluetooth, looked at me, and smiled sweetly. "It really is."

Then he slipped his hand onto my thigh and settled into his seat, and for the whole trip, we listened to Linkin fucking Park.

I'D ALWAYS ENJOYED the drive up to the Casa, but it was even better with Cooper. We chatted easily the entire way, and as the city thinned with the traffic, our scenery became more coastal. Though it used to relax me to come up here, the closer we got to our destination, the more anxious I became. I took the familiar road and when we were almost there, I turned the music off. "You nervous?" I asked him.

He looked surprised by my question. "No. Should I be?"

I smiled at his confidence. "I just don't think Sofia will be very understanding. No matter what she says, just remember, I'm on your side."

"Ryan's mom always liked me," he said.

"She likes you as Ryan's friend, yes," I told him. "But as my boyfriend..."

He shrugged. "And all the guys who'll be here this weekend?" he asked. "All Ryan's friends, some of my friends, they'll all be here too. We're meeting *them* as a couple too."

Shit. I hadn't given that a thought.

Then Cooper took his hand off my thigh and looked out the window as he spoke. "If you don't want to..."

I pulled the car off to the side of the road, right near the driveway to the Casa. I think I startled him. He looked at me, wide-eyed.

"Cooper, listen to me," I said seriously. "I don't care what anyone else thinks. I know some people will have a hard time with us being together because we're gay men, and because of the age difference. But I don't care. I'm proud to call you my boyfriend. For the life of me I can't figure out why you'd want to be with me, but you do, and I'm more than happy to walk in there, holding your hand. But I don't want you to feel pressured."

"I don't feel pressured," he said. "And I can't figure out why you'd want to be with me either, but you do."

I nodded. "Yes, I do."

He smiled, leaned over the console, and kissed me. "Thank you."

I sighed and looked out of the windshield. "Well, this is it."

Cooper followed my gaze to the stone gateposts, to the chiseled sandstone sign on the post that read Casa de Elkin.

"It's named after you?"

I nodded. "I designed this house," I told him. "We named it Casa de Elkin but have called it the Casa for years."

Cooper gave me a weak smile. "Well then," he said, trying to sound upbeat. "Let's do this."

I slipped the car into first gear and pulled into the drive. I parked near the closed garage doors, and by the time I'd popped the trunk, Ryan was walking out to meet us. He gave me a bit of a hug, then bumped fists with Cooper.

"Hey," he said. "Most of the guys will get here in the morning. Mom said it might be better if they all crash in the pool room or wherever they pass out," he said with a knowing smile. "But you guys have a guest room in the house."

A guest room.

Ryan looked at me a little apologetically. "Sorry."

"Don't you apologize," I told him. "It's not my house anymore."

We grabbed our bags and the gift box from the trunk and walked toward the front door. Cooper asked me quietly, "Have you been back here in the last five years?"

"I spent two weeks here right after we separated," I told him. "But not since then."

"Come on," Ryan said, opening the door. He turned to us and whispered, "Mom's in the kitchen."

I took a deep breath and followed Ryan through the front living room and into the large open kitchen, where Sofia was dicing fruit.

She looked well. She was wearing a white dress and her trademark gold jewelry, and her brown hair was pulled back in a ponytail. She looked at me, then at Ryan, and finally at Cooper. She recognized him immediately. "Oh my, Cooper? Is that you?"

"Mrs. Elkin," he said politely.

She gave me a tight smile but then leaned in and kissed Cooper's cheek. "It's so good to see you. Ryan never mentioned you were coming." Then she looked at me. "Did you bring Cooper with you? I thought you were bringing your friend."

There was a beat of absolute silence, then I said, "I did."

Sofia looked at me, then at Ryan and Cooper, then back to me.

"I brought Cooper... my boyfriend."

Sofia laughed, but when I took Cooper's hand, her smile died a slow, painful death. "Is this some kind of joke?"

"No," I said calmly. "Cooper and I have been together for about six weeks, and we... *dated* for six weeks before that."

Sofia took a step back from us, looking at the three of us, but her eyes settled on me. "You're *dating* Cooper?"

"Yes," I answered.

"No," she said flatly. "He's just a boy!"

Before I could answer, Cooper said, "Mrs. Elkin, I'm not a *boy*."

She stared at him. "Did he coerce you into this? Did he mislead you?"

"*What?*" Cooper and Ryan asked in unison.

"Sofia," I said. "That's enough—"

"Excuse me?" Cooper said, interrupting me. He was looking at Sofia, and I could tell by the set of his jaw, he was pissed off.

I considered asking both Cooper and Ryan to give Sofia and me a moment to talk alone, but she'd gone too far. She'd insulted Cooper.

"Actually, no," I said. "Cooper you don't need to excuse yourself or to apologize to anyone for anything." I took a step back, pulling him with me. "Sorry, Ryan, we'll find a hotel."

"No you won't," Ryan said, stopping us. "You're my guest, you can stay here. And, Mom," he said, looking at Sofia, "they're together. You need to deal with it." Then Ryan looked at Cooper and me. "Isn't that what you told me? I just had to deal with it?"

"Uh, pretty much," Cooper answered.

I felt a sudden rush of pride for Ryan. He defending me, probably more so to keep his parents from fighting and him being caught in the middle, but still... his stepping in was heart-warming.

"Wait!" Sofia cried, turning to Ryan. "You knew about this?"

"Yes," he replied slowly. "I was the one who told you about it, remember?"

"Sofia, it's certainly not Ryan's fault," I said.

She stared at me, long and hard, as though she couldn't understand. "Are there *no* men over forty-five in New York City?" Then she leaned back against the kitchen counter and groaned out a sigh. The fight in her was gone. "Really, Tom?"

I squeezed Cooper's hand. "Yes, really."

Sofia shook her head. She still wasn't happy, but at least she'd stopped yelling. She turned back to her chopping board and took a paring knife to a mango. "I was making a mango salsa to go with grilled chicken for dinner," she said. "I thought it would be nice food for company. I was trying to be supportive and show that I didn't have a problem with you bringing a friend."

"My *boyfriend*," I corrected her. "And I appreciate the sentiment, but we fell a little short on the welcome."

She put the knife down, which was probably a good thing. "How about a little warning, Tom? How about a phone call before you got here to say you're dating someone who went to school with our son?"

"Okay," I conceded. "Yes, I probably should have given you some warning. I apologize."

Cooper squeezed my hand.

Sofia sighed loudly, put both her hands on the kitchen counter, and took a breath. Then she faced us and tried to smile. "Apology accepted. Cooper, I'm very sorry for the way I spoke to you. I was taken off guard, and I'm sorry."

He gave her a curt smile. "It's fine, Mrs. Elkin." But it was clear to see it wasn't fine with him at all.

"We might go freshen up," I told her, giving us all some time to cool down. "Which of the guest rooms is ours?"

She stopped then and looked down, as though she finally realized I was staying here with someone else. "The blue room," she said quietly. "Second on the left."

All the guest rooms were upstairs, so I led Cooper back the way we'd come to the stairs in the foyer. I dropped his hand to pick up our suitcases, and he quietly followed me up to the room.

I put the bags at the foot of the bed, Cooper closed the door behind us, and I turned to face him. "I'm really sorry about that," I told him. "I didn't think she'd take it very well, but she seems to have calmed down a bit."

Cooper looked at me. "She might be your ex-wife, and she might be Ryan's mother, and I was taught to show respect," he said, "but she's a bitch."

I cupped his face in my hands and pecked his lips. "Yes, she was very rude."

"I was just about to tell her to mind her own fucking business," he went on to say. "I don't get angry very often, but she insinuated that you coerced me! Like you were some creeped-out pedophile and I was some innocent kid."

"I know," I agreed, but then he cut me off.

"And thank God you stood up for me," he said quickly, "telling her I didn't need to apologize to anyone for anything because I was just about to say something I'd probably have regretted."

I held his forehead to mine and took a deep breath. "You would've been well within your rights," I told him. "The fact she'd insulted you is what made me react."

He twisted his lips into a frowning pout. "Yes, she

assumed it was you who coerced me!" he sulked. "When it was *me* who coerced *you*!"

"The hide of her," I said with a smile. "Is there anything I can do to make it up to you?"

Still pouting, he pretended to have to think about it. "Well, she did hurt my feelings."

I cupped his balls in my hand. "Does it hurt here?" I asked against his lips. "Want me to kiss it better?"

He smiled. "Would it be considered rude if you were to suck me off with your ex-wife making us dinner downstairs?"

I pulled his bottom lip between my teeth and stroked his cock through his cargos. "Very rude."

He smiled. "Then yes, kiss it better," he said as he rubbed his dick against my hand.

I pushed him onto the bed and undid the fly on his cargos.

"Tom?"

I freed his cock from his briefs and looked up at him. "Yeah?"

"I think she hurt your feelings too," he said, leaning up on his elbows. "I think I might need to kiss yours while you kiss mine." Cooper pulled me onto the bed, and within seconds we were sixty-nineing, with our pants around our hips and our dicks down each other's throats.

At least that way Sofia couldn't hear him scream.

CHAPTER FOUR

DINNER WAS MUCH MORE RELAXED. Well, Cooper and I were much more relaxed after 'freshening up' upstairs. Sofia, on the other hand, seemed more resigned.

She was trying to make an effort. Conversation seemed to revolve around Ryan, which was fine, but she eventually asked Cooper about his parents, how they were and what they were doing. She asked him about his job and he answered politely. He could see she was making an effort and he extended the courtesy, though it was fairly obvious the damage was done.

Not long after dinner, Ryan wanted to know if he could open his birthday present. He'd been eyeing the wrapped gift box since I'd put it on the counter. "If everyone's arriving tomorrow, I won't have much time to enjoy it," he said. "Whatever it is."

Cooper grinned. "You're gonna love it."

"You know what it is?" Ryan asked him, and Cooper nodded. Ryan then looked at me. "Can I open it, pleeeeeease?" he whined like a five-year-old.

I said, "Yes, but take it into the living room."

Ryan all but raced to the living room with his present, while Cooper quietly thanked Sofia for dinner before joining Ryan in the living room. And no sooner had I picked up the finished plates and taken them to the kitchen than I heard the sound of paper ripping.

Then Ryan yelled from the other room, "Oh my fucking God!" He then appeared at the door holding the box. His grin was huge. "You didn't!"

"I did," I told him. "Direct from Japan. There are only a handful of them in the States until it's released in the fall apparently, so it wasn't exactly easy to get. Though it was Cooper's idea. You can thank him."

Ryan threw one arm around Cooper, hugging him in a man-hug kind of way. "Thanks, man!"

Cooper looked at him seriously, hopefully. "That means I can play too, right?"

They disappeared back into the living room, and I was still smiling when Sofia walked in with more dirty plates.

"Leave them," I told her. "I'll clean up."

She put them in the sink. "Your birthday gift was a hit."

"Yes, well, he mentioned he wanted it to Cooper," I told her as I filled the sink with hot water. "I wouldn't have known otherwise."

"Ryan and Cooper are still friends?" she asked.

"Yes, why wouldn't they be?"

She shook her head like I was missing the obvious.

"Look, Sofia, I'm not going to argue with you about him," I told her outright. "You offered for me to bring my partner, so I did. I'm not hiding anything anymore, Sofia. Would you prefer I lie to you? Would you prefer to find out from someone else?"

She exhaled loudly but didn't answer. Instead, she picked up a dishtowel and started to dry the plates. It was like she wanted to say something but kept stopping herself, and there was a heavy silence between us.

When we'd finished dish-duty, Sofia seemed to be back to resigned. "I'm turning in for the night. See you in the morning," she said, and without another word, she walked out.

I finished tidying up, checked my emails, watched and laughed at Ryan and Cooper for a while as they played a game I couldn't follow, but then told them I was heading to bed.

I stripped down to my briefs, climbed into bed, and closed my eyes. Not fifteen minutes later, warm hands slid around me and a familiar body pressed against me. Cooper whispered in my ear, "No sleep for you yet. I have somewhere else I need you to kiss better."

"Is that so?" I murmured.

"Mm-mm," he hummed. "But it's inside me... about eight inches inside me. I'm sure you can reach it."

I laughed into the pillow before I rolled over to kiss him. "I'm sure I can."

———————

COOPER AND I WOKE EARLY, and he decided we should take a walk along the beach, just the two of us, before our day was filled with other people.

He didn't have to say he wanted some time away from Sofia. I just understood. He held my hand as we walked. He was quiet, but he seemed happy. "I think we should take a swim when we get back to the house," he told me. "Then we can have breakfast, take another swim and maybe a nap before twenty of Ryan's friends turn up."

I stopped walking on the beach and pulled Cooper against me. I stared at him for a long moment before slowly sliding my hand along his jaw and kissing him. He melted against me, into me, and when I slid my tongue into his mouth, he moaned.

I finally pulled away from him, leaving him dazed. And smug. "What was that for?"

"A thank you," I told him. "For being here with me. For putting up with my ex-wife for a weekend. It's a lot to ask of you and I wanted you to know I'm grateful."

He took my hand and we started walking back to the house. "Well, you can show me how grateful you are by making me breakfast, and then how grateful you *really* are when we have a nap."

I was smiling as we walked back up to the house, still holding hands. Sofia had already put out a spread of croissants and fruit on the back patio table. She and Ryan were there and while Ryan smiled at us, Sofia quickly made the offer of coffee and walked inside.

She came back out a few minutes later with a tray of fresh coffee and some mugs, and to her credit, she did try to get along.

After we'd eaten, Cooper declared it was time for a swim. He and Ryan left me sitting at the table and went to get changed, but then Cooper came back and put his hands on my shoulders. He leaned down and spoke in my ear. "That includes you."

Sofia, who was picking a platter up off the table, cleared her throat. "You boys go and swim while I get things ready," she said, though she was clearly uncomfortable with public displays of affection between us.

I followed Cooper up the stairs and into our room. He was smiling, rather pleased with himself.

"I don't think Sofia appreciated you touching me," I told him as I was getting changed into my swimming shorts.

Cooper smiled. "That's why I did it."

I tried not to smile. "Be nice. She's trying to accept it. She'll be fine with us, you'll see."

He lifted one perfectly arched eyebrow. "Tom, are you blind?" he asked. "She's jealous! She wants you back!"

"No she doesn't," I replied quickly.

"Babe, she looks at you all the time. I'm telling you, she wants you."

"I don't want her." I tied off my shorts and crossed the room to him. "I don't want her. I don't want to go back. I've never been happier than where I am right now, okay?"

He nodded, then his lips curled into a slow smile. "Why do you always know what to say?"

"Years of experience."

Cooper sighed, then, changing the subject, he scrubbed his fingers along my unshaven jaw. "You look hot with scruff."

"My scruff, as you call it, is all gray along here," I admitted, rubbing my chin.

Cooper's hazel eyes scanned over my face. "And it's sexy as fuck," he said gruffly.

"Come on." I chose to ignore his comment and dragged him toward the door. "If you keep looking at me like that, we'll need to lock this bedroom door."

He laughed down the stairs. "I'm not opposed to that idea."

No, he never was.

WE SWAM in the pool for a while, and I caught Sofia watching us several times. I wondered if Cooper was right—whether Sofia did want me back. I mean, it had been five years. She'd dated other men, though none of them seriously.

Not that it mattered. I mean, it would be unfortunate for her, but I was *gay* and I'd never been happier than I was with Cooper.

He splashed me in the pool, then wrapped his arms around me, not caring who saw. "I think we're out of time for that little nap we were going to have," he said with a smile. "So you'll have to make it up to me tonight. I might be drunk later on, but you have my full consent to have your way with me."

I laughed, but then Sofia called out from inside the house, "Tom? I need you and Ryan to move some tables for me."

Cooper smiled knowingly. "She does know you're not married anymore, yes?"

I kissed him, slow and open-mouthed, knowing Sofia could see. I pulled his bottom lip in between my lips, making him smile. "Yeah, I think she knows," I told him. "Now we need to get out of this pool before we get too carried away."

So Cooper spent the next hour or so playing video games with Ryan while I moved tables and chairs, per Sofia's instructions.

And it wasn't long after that, the first cars of Ryan's friends started to arrive. Then the caterers turned up along with the waitstaff, so I told Cooper I was ducking upstairs to shower and change into something a little more appropriate. Of course he joined me, so it was maybe an hour later that we made it back downstairs.

There was quite a crowd gathered, a few faces I recognized, a lot I didn't. Cooper was right by my side when I stopped dead at some unexpected familiar faces.

Fuck.

My parents.

CHAPTER FIVE

"OH, TOM," my mother said warmly. She kissed my cheek. "So good to see you."

My father offered a handshake in greeting. "Son."

"Mom, Dad, I didn't know you'd be here." I was unable to hide my surprise.

"Oh," my mother said, "Sofia called us and asked us to come over."

Of course she had.

My parents didn't live too far from the Casa, so it wasn't too unreasonable that they be there. But still... they were my parents to invite, not hers.

I turned to Cooper and whispered, "My parents. Fuck, I'm so sorry."

But he never missed a beat. He said a polite hello to them as though he was interrupting so he could ask me where Ryan was. There was a loud peal of laughter outside, to which Cooper looked. "Never mind, found him," he said, and he disappeared outside.

I sat with them a while. They told me it was so nice of me to come and spend time with Sofia. My mom told me she'd always hoped we'd reconcile, then she smiled and patted my hand.

Sofia was there. She saw it. And she saw how much I fucking hated it. If she thought for one deluded moment this was some cruel trick to make me see how happy it would make my parents, then the look on my face must have set her fucking straight.

Thankfully my parents were oblivious to me glaring at my ex-wife and equally oblivious to how I looked for Cooper through the glass doors.

Sofia didn't miss that either.

My parents spent a quick ten minutes with Ryan but wanted to leave before the crowd got drunk and loud. I saw them out, walking them to their car, and told them I'd be in touch. I promised to call them during the week, and I would.

But as soon as they were heading down the drive, I went inside in search of Cooper. I found him through the crowd, drinking and laughing with some of his friends. I wasn't sure if I should walk up to him or just try to catch his eye. I didn't know what his friends knew or what they thought.

But he looked around, and when he saw me, he smiled and called me over. "Have they gone?" he said in front of his friends.

"Yeah, I'm really sorry," I told him. "I had no idea."

He slipped his arm around my waist, in front of his friends, in front of everyone. "It's okay," he said with a smile. Then he introduced me to his friends—who all *knew* I was Ryan's father—as his boyfriend.

They were all a little wide-eyed, but Cooper didn't seem to care. He squeezed my waist reassuringly and smiled, just as Ryan walked over to my other side and put his arm around my shoulder.

The four pairs of wide eyes in front of us then landed on Ryan, who simply raised his beer bottle at them. "Yep, I know they're dating," he said, then tapped his bottle to the closest guy. "I'm on empty. Your turn to get the birthday boy a beer, asswad."

And that was the end of that conversation.

By the quiet whispers and people looking at us, it didn't take long for the word to pass around the party crowd that Cooper and I were together. The fact we stood there with his arm around my waist kind of confirmed it. He was so open, so out and proud, so blasé to what others thought. And even though he was half my age, he was twice as brave as me. I stood by his side with his arm around me as he chatted with his friends, amazed by his confidence and the conviction of who he was.

As the night got later and as the music got louder, the more they drank, the more inclined I was to let him have a night with his friends. He was laughing and talking about college and people they knew, and every time I dropped my arm from around his waist to leave him to it, he'd tighten his hold on me.

So I stayed.

At least I avoided Sofia for the rest of the night. And at two in the morning, I helped carry a very drunk Cooper up the stairs and put him to bed. He was a very giggly, hug-everyone kind of drunk, and when I finally got him undressed and in bed, he was all smiles and slurred words I couldn't make out. It was kind of cute.

His snoring wasn't so likable.

NEEDLESS TO SAY, I was up long before any of the

bodies strewn across the house, so I decided to make a start on cleaning up. I had a few trash bags full of bottles and cans by the time Sofia ventured out. I avoided her. I was still too mad at her, and she seemed equally pleased to avoid me.

But one by one the partygoers woke up, drank coffee, and went on their way. I fed both Cooper and Ryan coffee and greasy bacon rolls until they felt better, and by mid-morning, they decided a cool swim would help with their hangovers.

Unfortunately it left me alone with Sofia.

"I think we need some coffee," she said, walking to the coffee machine. "Want a cup?"

"Sure," I told her. "Why not."

She poured two cups, handed me one, then stood leaning against the kitchen counter. She was quiet for a while, so I asked her about her sisters and told her I liked the new pieces of furniture I'd seen around the Casa. She asked how my work was going, how Jennifer was, and we talked about mutual friends.

Then she said, "I'm sorry about asking your parents to come last night." She even had the decency to look it.

"You should be, Sofia. I'm sorry to say it like that, but it wasn't your place to invite my parents."

"I thought they'd like to see Ryan for his birthday."

"And you thought you'd like to show Cooper that my parents don't know what he is to me."

"That's not what I meant to do."

"Yes, it is."

Conversation had never been a problem for us, though now it was very strained. There was an obvious elephant in the room.

Well, the metaphorical elephant who was taking a swim with Ryan.

It was obvious she wanted to say something about him, but she wasn't sure how to bring it up. Then there was a burst of laughter from the pool, Cooper's laughter, and it made me smile.

"You seem genuinely taken with him."

"I am."

"How did you meet?" she asked me quietly. "I mean, this time. How did you meet... again."

"Through Ryan initially," I told her. "But then he had an internship at the office. That's where I got to know him."

"You worked with him?"

"Yes."

"But he doesn't work with you now?"

"No, he works for Arlington. He fits in better there. They're young and innovative."

"And Brackett and Golding are an old prestigious classic," she said. "How ironic."

I ignored the jibe. "He's really very talented," I told her. "He'll go a long way."

Sofia nodded. "He will if he stays with you," she said. "Riding on the coattails of the great Thomas Elkin will get him anywhere."

I put my coffee on the counter with a clunk, probably a little louder than I intended to. I tried to keep my voice down. "It's not like that. That's the very reason I told him to work somewhere else, so he wouldn't be associated with me professionally. He'll go far because he's talented, Sofia, not because of who he's with."

"Tom, forgive me for not understanding the connection between you," she said with hard eyes. "But have you thought of the possibility he could be after your money?"

Anger swelled in my chest, but I tamped it down. She was acting all concerned, but really she wanted to make me angry. She wanted to get a reaction out of me, so I refused to give her one.

"He's not after money, Sofia, and I find it offensive that you imply he is," I said as calmly as I could manage.

"How do you know, Tom?"

"I know he's not after my money because I asked him to move in with me, and he said no."

She stared at me for a long moment. "You asked him to move in with you?"

"Yes," I said with a smile of satisfaction. "And he turned me down."

"Well, at least one of you is thinking clearly."

"Oh, give it up, Sofia." I turned to walk out.

"You give it up, Tom," she said, stopping me. "It's embarrassing. You're making a fool of yourself."

"I don't care, Sofia. I don't care what you think or what anyone else thinks. I care what Cooper thinks."

"I don't get it," she said, shaking her head. "I don't understand what you could possibly have in common. He's half your age!"

"You *wouldn't* understand, Sofia," I said, probably too loudly. "He understands me. He *gets* me. The age difference doesn't come into it at all. I'm sorry you don't get it, but you don't have to. What we have is between Cooper and me, and no one else. It's no one else's fucking business."

Sofia opened her mouth to say something, but I'd heard enough.

"I love him, Sofia." It was the first time I'd said those words out loud. I'd thought them a hundred times but never had the courage to say them, to admit them. "You and I won't ever get back together, if that's what you're aiming for here. Beside the fact that *I'm gay*, Sofia, I am in love with Cooper. I *love* him."

Sofia paled as though my words had found their mark, but her eyes darted past me, over my shoulder. I followed her gaze to see Cooper standing at the back patio doors, looking directly at me.

He was still wet from the pool, shirtless, with a beach towel wrapped around his waist. He blinked a few times before he walked inside.

"Cooper," Sofia said, but he put his hand up to stop her talking as he walked over to me.

My heart was hammering. My stomach was in knots. He'd heard everything. He stood in front of me and shook his head. "Oh, Tom, you've done it again."

I could barely speak. "Done what?"

"Gone and spoken to someone else about how you feel about me," he said. His hair was wet and drops of water ran down his body, but he didn't seem to care. He stared right at me. "Don't you think that's something you should have told me first?"

I nodded quickly, petrified of what he might say.

Cooper bit his lip and slowly shook his head. "First you tell Louisa that you want something more with me, and now you tell your ex-wife, of all people, that you love me?"

"I keep getting it wrong. I should have told you."

Cooper looked over at Sofia, who was watching us with a look of dismay on her face, then he turned back to me and he smiled. She'd been blatantly horrible to him, and he wanted me to say this in front of Sofia. He wanted her to see that I was choosing him. "So tell me now."

It was the first time I'd seen him be remotely possessive. It was the first time I'd seen fear in his eyes. There was a bead of water threatening to fall from his hair, so I touched it and pressed my palm to his face. My words were barely a whisper. "I love you, Cooper. I'm *in* love with you," I told him, and he smiled beautifully. Then I told him, "You drive me crazy, you drive me crazy some days, and you challenge everything I say, but you've breathed life into me. I never expected someone could understand me like you do."

He smiled sweetly, then whispered, "Thank you," before he pressed his lips to mine.

Sofia made some sound that was a half-scoff, half-sigh, and Cooper smiled against my lips. "I think we should go back to New York."

"I think that's a good idea," Sofia said softly.

Ten minutes later we were packed, we'd said our good-byes to Ryan—though he said he'd see us next week some-time—Sofia had bid us a quiet, distant farewell, and we were on the road.

Cooper was pensive, but he took my hand and smiled. It wasn't lost on me that he'd not returned any declaration of love—he'd simply thanked me for mine.

But he was radiating happiness, even hungover. I didn't think he'd stopped smiling yet. Even when he fell asleep in the car, he was smiling.

The quiet drive, with Cooper sleeping in the passenger seat, gave me some time to think.

I didn't regret what I'd told him.

I didn't regret saying it in front of Sofia.

I regretted none of it.

I didn't expect him to tell me he loved me back. I realized when I was driving back to the City that it didn't matter. It only mattered that he knew I loved him.

And when we'd arrived back at my apartment, a still-sleepy Cooper dropped his suitcase inside my front door and went and raided the fridge.

I leaned against my kitchen counter and watched as he mumbled to himself and pulled out two sodas. "Want one?"

he asked, but then his smile faltered. He closed the fridge and stood in front of me. "Tom, babe, what's wrong?"

"Nothing," I answered. "Nothing at all."

"You're looking at me funny," he said, but he looked concerned. "Is it because you said you loved me and I didn't say anything back?"

I hushed him, then pressed my lips to his.

"What is it?"

"Take me to bed," I whispered.

He looked at me for a long moment. "Okay," he agreed, but he was worried.

"No, Cooper." I held his face and shook my head. "I want you to take me to bed," I repeated. He still looked confused, so I spelled it out for him. "Cooper, I want you to top me."

CHAPTER SIX

"ARE YOU SURE?" he asked.

I was naked on the bed and he was kneeling between my thighs.

"Yes. I am," I told him, again. He'd asked me in the kitchen, he'd asked me before we undressed, now he was asking again. "I'm very sure. I want to share this with you."

He exhaled with a nervous laugh. "I don't want to hurt you."

He knew I'd never bottomed, he knew this was new territory for me, so he understood how much this meant.

I sat up and swiped the pad of my thumb across his bottom lip. "Take your time and you won't hurt me."

He kissed me then, and we fell back onto the bed. He slicked his fingers and probed my ass while he probed my mouth with his tongue. He was gentle and sweet, he took his time, and he took care of me.

He licked and sucked my cock while he slid his fingers inside me over and over, stretching me, preparing me for him. For where I wanted him. He pressed my gland again and again while he worshiped my cock with his mouth.

The intensity of my orgasm was crippling and amazing. I'd never felt anything like it. I'd never come so hard. It was like he'd rendered my bones to liquid. I heard the rip of foil, then he pushed my legs up to my chest.

I was pliable, like Jell-O. And I still wanted more.

When he pressed against me and pushed inside, it was a stretch and a burn, but he was slow and careful, and I welcomed it.

He leaned over me while he oh-so-slowly filled me, giving me time to adjust. I put my arms around his neck and watched him. I watched his eyes roll back, I watched him tremble, his chest rise and fall in rapid breaths, and I watched as he licked his lips and whimpered.

His pleasure was mine.

He kissed me, he gave me his tongue, he pulled on my bottom lip, and he kissed me again. Then his thrusts got a little harder and a little deeper, and he groaned long and low.

"Tom," he whispered gruffly. Then cupped my face and his lips ghosted mine as he breathed, as he thrust into me. He said my name again, and I lifted my legs higher, and he flexed into me as he came.

Completely spent, he collapsed on me, and I traced circles on his back until he'd caught his breath. He pulled out of me, kissed me tenderly, then he cleaned me up.

He never said a word.

But when he climbed back onto the bed, he wrapped his arms and legs around me. He'd never held me so tight.

We spent the afternoon in bed, alternating between sleep and making out. When I was on top of him, kissing his neck and jaw, I rolled us over so he was on top of me, and I asked him to make love to me again.

He made me come again with no less intensity than

before, then he laid me face down on the bed. He pressed his weight on me, then pressed inside me. He threaded his fingers with mine and whimpered and moaned in my ear. He kissed the back of my neck and shoulder as he slowly thrust into me. His weight on me, his breath hot in my ear, and his teeth scraping my skin set my body on fire. I raised my ass to meet him, to give more of me to him, and his whole body convulsed when he came.

I'd never heard him moan like that.

He collapsed again on top of me, keeping his weight on me. He pulled out of me but continued to rock his hips a little and murmur, "Fuck, baby," over and over.

Eventually we left the bed and showered, and Cooper ordered dinner. We sat on the sofa and ate our takeout, and he was telling me a funny story of something that happened at work. He made me laugh—like he always made me laugh—and I was still chuckling when I speared some of his lemon chicken and shoved it in my mouth.

When I looked up at him, he was quiet and looking at me funny. So with a mouth half-full of food, I said, "What's wrong? I'm allowed to steal some of your dinner. You ate half of mine."

He smiled slowly. "I love you."

I almost forgot to swallow my food and somehow managed not to choke. "Huh?"

"Do you need hearing aids, old man?" he said with a grin. "I said I love you."

"No, I don't need hearing aids." Then I giggled. I think I even blushed.

Cooper leaned over the Chinese food and kissed me with smiling lips, then just carried on his conversation about his co-worker like nothing extraordinary had happened.

Except it had.

He loved me. He'd said so. Twice.

He told me he'd had one of the best days of his life, but he said he needed to go home—he had to be at work early and had no work clothes here. I called him a cab and kissed him at the door. "You could always move in," I said again.

He rolled his eyes. "We've been through that," he said and gave me a quick peck on the lips, then walked toward the elevator with his suitcase.

"And you turned me down," I called out down the hall.

He pressed the button. "I did," he said, looking back at me with a cheeky grin. "Because you asked me all wrong," he added, then stepped inside the elevator, and the door closed.

I asked him all wrong. What the hell did that mean? I gave him about twenty minutes to get home and settled, then I sent him a text.

What do you mean I asked you all wrong?

His response took less than a minute. *Aren't you in bed yet, old man?*

I replied, *I'm not old, thank you very much. But I won't sleep if you don't tell me.*

Are you sore? Do you feel okay?

I've never felt better, thank you.

You're very welcome. And thank you for a great weekend and an amazing day.

You didn't answer my question.

You noticed.

Cooper, I need to know. How did I ask you wrong?

Because you didn't ask me right.

You like to challenge me, don't you?

You said it was one of the things you loved about me.

I smiled at my phone, but quickly typed back, *It is. Goodnight, Tom. WYWH.*

I had to Google what the acronym was, and before I could reply, another message came through.

Did you just Google that?

Little smart ass. *Shut up. Yes, I did. And you wouldn't have to wish I was there if you moved in with me.*

LOL. Oh but Tom, you're asking all wrong again.

I sighed. *Goodnight Cooper.*

Goodnight Tom. ILY.

Just as I smiled at my phone another message came through. *That means I love you.*

I gathered that much, smart-ass.

I think we'll need to work on your terms of endearment.

I shook my head and laughed. I doubted I'd ever win with him. *ILY.*

ILY2.

JENNIFER GREETED me with her usual morning message update and the reassurance of hot coffee on my desk. Then she smiled warmly at me. "You look refreshed. I trust you had a good weekend?"

"My weekend was wonderful," I told her.

"How was Sofia?" Jennifer knew everything there was to know about me, and she knew my ex-wife had met my boyfriend over the weekend.

"Well, she wasn't overly impressed, no." I shrugged. "But we had a lovely time. Ryan loved his gift, so thank you for helping me with that."

She smiled. "My pleasure."

"Well, considering I had the weekend off, I'd better get to it," I told her.

"Yes, looks like a busy week." She was back to her

professional best. "I'll give you twenty minutes to check emails and then we can discuss your weekly schedule."

"Thank you, Jennifer." I walked into my office.

I checked emails, responding to anything urgent, then Jennifer and I mapped out the next two weeks' worth of appointments, meetings, and deadlines. It was busy, and I knew there'd be work to take home.

Cooper was in the same predicament. His schedule was as busy as mine, though he'd bring work to my place instead of his, and we'd work at my dining table. Most nights that week, we spent hours in a peaceful silence as we worked, though we'd stop for 'intermission' as Cooper called it. Which was dinner and sex.

Not always intercourse, but a blow job or mutual hand jobs on the sofa, sometimes too worked up to even get undressed. He was insatiable, completely voracious.

Not that I minded. Hell, I was starting to want it as much as he did.

We were getting cozy on the sofa when I told him of my busy schedule, how I'd be working most of the weekend to get a big contract finalized, and he said he didn't mind.

"I've got some work I can bring over," he said. "I'll be really quiet and won't interrupt you, I promise."

I threw my head back and laughed. "Oh, please," I said. "You can't help yourself. As soon as you get bored, I become a source of entertainment."

He grinned, pushed me back on the sofa and proceeded to unzip my pants and lick and suck me, which proved my point exactly.

But on Saturday, when we'd been working for a few hours, he had his head down going over plans he'd brought with him and hadn't interrupted me once. It was driving me insane. I *wanted* him to interrupt me.

And it was so typically Cooper to *not* interrupt me because I'd made a point of saying he would.

Always challenging.

By lunchtime, I couldn't stand it. I'd spent the last hour staring at him, trying to get his attention, and of course he knew. He was trying not to smile. When I got up from the table and pulled out his chair, swinging my leg over and straddling him, he burst out laughing.

"You're such a tease," I told him before pushing his head back and kissing him hard.

When I pulled my mouth from his, he licked his lips. "I wondered how long it would take," he said smugly. "You've got some pretty good self-control." He gripped my hips and rocked me on his lap. "It's been killing me."

I ground down on him. "Your self-control is apparently better than mine," I said, before kissing him again. "Just take me to bed."

I'd never imagined I'd bottom. I'd never imagined I'd want to. But giving myself to him that way was something special. The way he worshiped my body before sinking inside me, the way my body gave him pleasure was empowering.

Since declaring our love, sex was even more intense between us. Everything was more intense—conversations, laughter, touches, and even the way we looked at each other.

I told Cooper that I'd spoken to my parents during the week. I'd promised I'd phone them and had arranged to drive up and see them next month. "I'm thinking I should tell them I've met someone," I explained. It was early afternoon. We were in bed, naked, wrapped up in each other.

Cooper leaned up on his elbows to look at me. "You're going to come out to them?"

I sighed. "I think so," I said. "I want to tell them. I want to tell them I found someone who makes me happy, that I've never been happier."

"But you're worried about how they'll react?" he asked.

"Yeah, of course," I admitted.

"I'll go with you," he said with a kind smile.

"Would you?" I asked. "I mean, I'd love to have you by my side. I want them to meet you. But you certainly don't have to."

"I don't have to. I want to."

"Anyway, it's a few weeks away," I told him. "We're both busy here, and we have that bloody concert next week-end," I said, rolling my eyes. But then I rolled us over so we faced each other and ran my hands through his hair. "Is it crazy that I'm considering coming out to my parents? I mean, I'm *forty-four* years old!"

Cooper smiled. "Not at all, Tom. It's not crazy. You still want their approval."

"Well, I'm fairly certain I won't get it." I tried to smile. "But I can hope, right?"

He pecked my lips. "Why are you doing it then? If you know they won't approve and it will cause problems, and you said it yourself, you don't need their approval, then why?"

"I don't want any secrets with them. And I want them to know I'm happy. I'm not expecting them to be accepting of it, or even tolerable. They'll more than likely choose to pretend I never told them and keep wishing I'll get back with Sofia."

Cooper snorted. "Maybe you should just tell them you're gay first before you drop the 'oh, and I'm seeing a twenty-two-year-old' bomb."

I laughed and pecked his lips again. "I may as well hit

them with both bombs. They won't take it well no matter which I tell them."

Cooper sighed and nipped at the skin on my chin. "Tom?"

"Yeah?"

"We'll need to keep one weekend free." Then he bit his lip. "How're your self-defense skills?"

I laughed. "Why?"

"I want you to meet my parents," he answered. "And I'm pretty sure your parents are gonna take it a helluva lot better than mine."

CHAPTER SEVEN

WELL, shit.

"They won't like the idea, huh?"

"Um, your birthday's in November, right?"

"Yeah, why?"

"Well, my dad's birthday is December..."

It took me a second. "I'm older than your dad?"

Cooper laughed and nodded. "Is that weird?"

Weird. That was one word to describe it. "Um, yes." I didn't know why it threw me so much. Our age difference had always been a glaring issue, but I'd come to accept it, ignore it. Yes, I was older than him. So what?

But I was also older than his *father*?

"Hey," Cooper said, putting his hand to my face. "It doesn't change anything."

"Doesn't it?"

"Does it change how you feel about me?" he asked calmly.

"No, of course not," I said quietly.

"Then it doesn't change anything."

There wasn't anything but absolute certainty in his

hazel eyes. I smiled and asked him, "How did you get so wise?"

"I'm just smart like that."

I kissed him with smiling lips. "You're just smug like that."

"It's a Gen-Y thing?"

"It's a Cooper-Jones thing," I said. "Did you still want me to meet your parents?"

"Yes," he said adamantly. "They know I'm seeing someone. They know it's serious, and they know his name is Tom. But that's all I've told them."

"You told them about me?" I couldn't help but smile.

"Of course I did," he said simply. "Just not exactly who *Tom* was. But if we're *that* serious, they should meet you."

"Then I'll meet them. Again," I clarified, "because I met them years ago, but I was only Ryan's dad back then, not their son's boyfriend."

Cooper chuckled. "They're gonna freak."

"And this is funny because...?"

He sighed and rolled onto his back. "Well, it's not really," he said. "But what else can I do? I've fallen in love with you, and if gender doesn't matter, then neither should age."

I leaned up on my arm and stared at this remarkable man. "You're incredible, you know that?"

He grinned at me. "Actually, yeah. I do know that." He sighed happily. "But you can keep telling me."

"I might have to write little notes, so I remember. You know, my Alzheimer's is getting bad."

Cooper laughed. "Oh my God! Thomas Elkin just made a joke! And it was even funny!"

"Shut up, you little shit."

He leaned up and kissed me. "See? I can go from 'incredible' to 'little shit' in two seconds. It's a talent."

I chuckled at him and pushed him to the side of the bed. "Well then, you incredible little shit, go and look up flights to Chicago, a rental car, and a hotel."

"I will," he said, getting off the bed and pulling on his pants. "If you organize dinner. I'm starving."

I watched him walk out of the bedroom and shook my head, still in disbelief that he was mine. Smiling, I pulled on my jeans and followed him out to the living room. He was clicking away at some flight website, so while I scrolled through restaurant phone numbers on my phone, I asked, "Steak, seafood, pasta? Your choice."

"Steak," came his quick reply, so I hit the number on my cell and made reservations for dinner.

Cooper waited for me to click off the call. "Are we going out?"

"Yes. You wanted steak."

He smiled warmly at me, then looked back at the laptop. "So which dates are better for you?"

Between us, we determined we had something going on for the next five weeks. We had that blasted concert, work, a trip to see his parents, then a trip to see mine, more work, and Cooper had an energy convention in Philly that Louisa had been priming him for.

I pulled my credit card from my wallet and put it beside him.

"What's that for?"

"To pay for the trip to Chicago." I kissed the top of his head.

He started to object my offer, but I leaned down and gently put my lips to his. "Please, Cooper. Let me do this for you."

His lips formed a twisted frown. "Are you sure? I hate that you can pay for things I can't. I feel like a kept boy."

"Of course I'm sure. And you're not a *kept* anything. The only thing you *keep* is me on my toes."

He huffed and gave me a small smile. I poured us both a juice while he paid for the trip to Chicago, and when he walked over to me to give me back my card, he slid his arms around me and nestled his face into my neck. "Thank you."

"You're very welcome," I replied with a kiss to the side of his head. "If it would make you feel any better, you can pay for dinner."

I felt him smile against my skin. "I don't feel *that* kept."

I chuckled and dug my fingers into his sides, tickling him. "Too bad, Mr. Jones. You're paying."

"Let me guess, you made reservations at some ridiculously over-priced restaurant."

"No, Perry's bar and grill. Next block over," I said with a smile. "Huge steaks, low prices. All the fries you can eat."

Cooper groaned. "Mr. Elkin, you know me so well."

"Yeah, well," I said, "I'll be having the steak and salad because my forty-four-year-old arteries aren't as forgiving as yours."

He cupped my balls in his hand and gave a gentle squeeze. "Your circulation works just fine."

I turned him around and slapped his ass. "Go, get dressed, or we'll be late."

He walked to the hall, rubbing his ass. "I can't believe you slapped me." Then he stood there and undid his pants, letting them slide down to his thighs, and he rubbed his naked ass. "I think you might need to kiss it better."

"After dinner," I said. "I'll do more than that."

He laughed when I had to adjust the front of my jeans.

The little shit.

WORK WAS hectic the next week. Hectic, but good. Cooper was just as busy, and I only saw him on Wednesday night when I went to his apartment and Friday night when he came to mine. We spent the night finalizing some work, then crashed in front of the TV.

The next morning, I asked him if he missed going out with the boys because he didn't do it very often. "I don't mind going out every once and a while," he reassured me. "But I'd prefer to be here. I like quiet nights in, too."

"I just don't want you to miss out on being twenty-two, that's all."

"I'm not missing out on anything. I spent four years at college not missing out on much, I can assure you."

"I'd rather not hear the details of that, thanks."

He chuckled and kissed me. "Anyway, we're going out tonight, are we not?"

I rolled my eyes. "We are."

He laughed when I told him one of the other senior partners, Robert Chandler—an esteemed New York architect, who had mentored me ten years ago—had assumed Linkin Park was a period-drama play because he wanted to know which theater on Broadway it was showing. "He thought it sounded Presidential."

Cooper laughed. "You work with dinosaurs."

I corrected him. "We're very talented, prestigious dinosaurs, thank you very much." Then I teased him, "Aren't you glad you weren't *his* intern?"

Cooper nodded and bit his bottom lip. "Yeah, I wouldn't have fantasized about being pushed against *his* drafting board, letting him have his wicked way with me..."

Forgetting what it was I was reading, I looked up and stared at him. "Fantasized? *My drafting board?*"

Cooper sat on the armrest of the sofa and smirked that

smug, salacious smile at me. "You'd make me face the board and I'd hold onto the top of it with my pants around my ankles. You wouldn't even bother to undo the button on your suit pants... just the zipper..."

I got up from the dining chair and walked over to stand between his legs, pressing myself against him.

Cooper smiled and his voice was gruff and slow. "And you'd fuck me."

"Jesus, Cooper," I said, pushing my hips against his, and he ran his hands over my ass. He could feel how hard I was. "I just can't get enough of you."

"Good," he whispered. "Because I want you all the time."

I kissed him, filling his mouth with my tongue. He pulled my hips harder into his, but I wedged my hand between us. I undid the button and fly on his cargos first, then on mine until our hardened cocks were pressed together. I gripped us both in one hand, still tongue-fucking his mouth while I jerked us off together. His cock was hot and silky-hard against mine.

He groaned in my mouth, and I needed air. I tugged my mouth from his and sucked back a breath, only to scrape my teeth down his jaw to his ear. "I'd fuck you so hard," I whispered in his ear. His head fell back and his cock surged and swelled in my hand.

Watching him come, feeling his warmth erupt over his stomach and down my hand, down my cock, brought me over the edge, and I shot white stripes over his skin.

He wrapped his arms around me and we slid over the armrest of the sofa, landing in a sticky mess with me lying on top of him.

The room still hadn't stopped spinning when Cooper chuckled underneath me.

"Fuck, Tom," he murmured. "That was intense."

"You shouldn't talk about fantasies like that," I mumbled into his neck.

He laughed again. "I think I really should talk about them more often." He ran his hands over my back and through my hair. "We should get cleaned up for tonight."

I noticed then that he still had one leg bent over the back of the sofa and his other foot on the ground while I was lying awkwardly over him. "I don't want to move. Too comfortable."

He chuckled. "Is this some old person yoga position? The dual pretzel?"

I laughed as I leaned up off him. "The sticky dual pretzel."

We untangled ourselves, and Cooper suggested we shower together. "To save water," he said. "We should be responsible, ecologically sound citizens," he said.

I rolled my eyes. "You just want to see me wet and naked, don't you?"

He laughed and put his wrist to his mouth, pretending to speak into some covert-operative mouthpiece. "My cover's been blown, I repeat, my cover's been blown."

"You're such a smart ass."

"Yeah, well," he said, pulling me into the bathroom. "You love me and my smart ass."

"Yes, I do."

Once we were out of the shower, dressed and almost ready to go, the intercom buzzed. Lionel's familiar voice said, "Mr. Elkin?"

I walked over and pressed the intercom button. "Yes, Lionel?"

"Sir, sorry to interrupt, but Ryan's on his way up."

That was odd. "Okay, that's fine, Lionel."

"Um, Mr. Elkin?"

"Yes?"

"Your ex-wife is with him."

"Sofia?"

"Yes, sir," he replied. "Just thought you'd like a little... notice."

Cooper walked up beside me and leaned into the intercom. "Lionel?"

"Mr. Jones?"

"You're worth more money."

The doorman laughed. "Just doing my job, sir."

Right then, there was a knock at the door. Cooper looked at me and smiled. "I'll do the honors."

CHAPTER EIGHT

"HEY," Cooper greeted Ryan as he opened the door.

"Hey, man," Ryan returned the sentiment.

Cooper stood to the side, gesturing for them to come in. "Mrs. Elkin," he said politely.

"Hello, Cooper." Sofia walked in slowly, looking as uncomfortable as I'd ever seen her. She'd only been to my place once or twice before, and it seemed she found Cooper being here a little off-putting.

I gave her a light kiss on the cheek. "What do we owe the pleasure?"

Not missing my use of the word 'we,' Sofia glanced at Cooper. "I was in town with Ryan and thought I'd stop by, if that's okay. Last time we saw each other, we didn't exactly leave on very happy terms." She quickly looked at Cooper again.

"No, we didn't," I agreed. But she didn't apologize, and I certainly wasn't about to either. "And it's fine for you to stop by, Sofia." I was going to add that a bit of notice would have been ideal but figured I'd take her olive branch for what it was. The fact Cooper was here, and even felt at home enough to open the door for them, should have been enough just desserts, but just in case it wasn't, I added, "Though we were actually just heading out."

"Where you guys going?" Ryan asked, looking up from the inside of the fridge.

"Madison Square Garden," Cooper answered with a grin.

Ryan stood up and gaped at him. "No freakin' way!" he cried. "Linkin Park?"

Then Sofia looked at me. "You're going to see Linkin Park?"

"I am," I told her. "Cooper puts up with my taste in music, so it's only fair that I put up with his."

"Yeah, that's true," Cooper agreed. "But my taste in music is awesome. Tom's is crap."

Ryan laughed, and I rolled my eyes. From the look on her face, it was obvious Sofia wasn't sure what to make of it, or of me and Cooper. He sat on the sofa and pulled on his shoes, then disappeared down the hall and came back with my boots.

"Thanks," I said quietly, taking my boots from him. As I pulled them on, I asked if Ryan and Sofia wanted to walk down with us, basically telling them we were leaving.

The elevator ride was quiet, but when we got to the lobby, Cooper snatched up my hand. It wasn't until we walked past Lionel that Cooper gave him a bit of a wave. "Thanks again, Lionel."

"My pleasure, Mr. Jones," he replied with a smile.

It was then Sofia turned around and saw that we were holding hands. She looked away quickly and pretended not to care, but she pursed her lips in that not-impressed way she always did.

I told Ryan to come over one night, Cooper told him to

bring his new Xbox, we bid Sofia a good night, then hailed a cab. Standing on the sidewalk with Sofia was awkward, and as soon as the cab pulled up, Cooper and I climbed in.

Cooper laughed. "She hates me."

I gave the taxi driver directions, then said, "Don't let her get to you."

"Hmm," he hummed. "Did you see her face when I opened your front door?"

"I don't think she expected you to open the door, that's for sure."

"You know," he said, squeezing my hand, "I normally can't stand it when someone doesn't like me. It annoys me until I find out why or until I break them down."

"Like Lionel," I added.

"Exactly. Now he loves me," he said simply. "But with Sofia, I just don't care. She can hate me all she likes."

I smiled at him. "I don't think she hates you. You were right—she's jealous."

"Which is irrational," he said. "It's not like I'm a young, blonde woman for her to compare herself to, or someone she could see herself twenty years ago as..."

"No," I conceded, "but I don't want her. I want you."

He smiled. "I know you do." He seemed placated a little. "And that's what she doesn't like."

"Can we not talk about my ex-wife?" I asked. "I'm spending the night with you, going to some god-forsaken concert."

Cooper smiled. "And it's gonna be freakin' awesome!"

THE CONCERT itself wasn't too bad. Though I didn't want to admit that to Cooper. I was by far the oldest person there from what I could tell, but Cooper didn't seem to notice. I watched him dance and sing almost every word. I watched him get pushed and shoved, and he never stopped smiling.

He loved it.

And that was what I went for.

My ears were ringing when we got home, and even when I woke up the next day. Cooper swore the only thing to get rid of the ringing in my ears would be to give him a blow job. He tried to reason that the sucking and swallowing motion would help pop the inner ear. Either that, or make him breakfast. He was pretty sure either would work.

Or both.

The little shit.

He left my apartment on Sunday afternoon, and when I got to work on Monday, I had a text from him saying if I still had ringing in my ears, he could come past the office, I could suck him off then buy him lunch, and that might help.

I typed out my reply, *It didn't help for breakfast or lunch yesterday. Why would today be any different?*

Maybe we need to do it two days in a row. Just to be sure. For medicinal research purposes, of course.

Of course.

Is that a yes?

No. Aren't you supposed to be working?

Very productive morning. Apparently two blow jobs yesterday was good for creativity.

I laughed at my phone. *Will I see you this week?*

Maybe Wednesday? he answered. *And I'll stay over on Friday before we leave for Chicago.*

Okay. I'll just sleep in my big bed alone...

Are you pouting?

Yes. And looking at my drafting board, imagining you bent over it...

Jesus, Tom... That's not fair.

See you Wednesday. LY.

There was no immediate reply, but after lunch my phone beeped, and I smiled when I saw his name. *No more sexting at work. I've had a hard-on all day.*

That's a shame, I replied, *because I ordered a drafting board to be delivered to my place this evening.*

His response was almost immediate. *I'll be there after work.*

I chuckled to myself, threw my phone into my drawer, and spent the next few hours getting some work done. I had actually ordered a new drafting board and asked for a six o'clock delivery to my apartment, so by five-thirty, I was finishing off some financials when Jennifer buzzed me.

"Sorry to interrupt you, Mr. Elkin," she said. "Sofia Elkin is on line one."

I groaned, and Jennifer simply asked, "Would you like me to take a message?"

"No," I said with a sigh. "I'll take it." I pressed the blinking button. "Sofia?"

"Yes, Tom," she answered. "I didn't want to call your personal line. I hope that's okay?"

I repressed another sigh. "That's fine. What are you calling for? Is everything okay?"

This time she sighed. "Yes, everything's okay. I just wanted to speak to you. I'm sorry I stopped by on Saturday unannounced." Then she asked, "How was the concert?"

"It was okay." Then making a point of calling him by name, I said, "But I wouldn't tell Cooper that. He'd make me go to another one."

"Right."

Sofia was quiet then, so I prompted her, "You said you wanted to speak to me?"

"Well, I just wanted to speak to you... without him being there..."

"Him?" I asked, failing to keep the bite from my tone. "You mean Cooper?"

"Tom, please don't be mad. I'm trying here."

"Well, you can start by calling him by his name."

"Can I see you over the weekend sometime? Without Cooper being there? Is that okay?"

She was unbelievable. "I can't this weekend. We're going to Chicago."

"Oh."

"So Cooper can introduce me to his parents. And the weekend after that, I'm taking him to meet my mom and dad, Sofia."

There was a long silence, then she said, "You're really doing this, aren't you?"

I wanted to tell her that I was *with* him, that I loved him, but I didn't. There wasn't any point. Instead, I told her, "Sofia, in the last five years, I've spoken to you a handful of times, and now that I've finally found someone, you've called me three times in two weeks. Sofia, you can call me about Ryan anytime, day or night, but if you're trying to cause problems, then I think the calls should stop."

There was complete silence.

So, to soften the blow, I said, "How about I give you a call in a few weeks and we can go out for coffee? I want you to get to know Cooper. I want you to see how wonderful he is, but you never will until you stop seeing him as some kind of threat."

"Okay."

"Sofia, I want you in my life," I told her honestly. "I

want us to be friends. I do. I know I hurt you, and I'm sorry for that. I truly am. But if you fight me on this, on Cooper, I will choose him."

When she didn't reply, I told her I had to go, but I'd be in touch in a few weeks. I put the receiver in the cradle, closed my files, shoved my laptop into my briefcase and left.

NEEDLESS TO SAY, the new drafting board was impressive.

So was Cooper.

He eyed the new addition to the living room somewhat cautiously. He bit his bottom lip and walked over to it, touching it reverently. "It's beautiful."

"It's a nineteen-twenties antique," I explained. "Solid oak, cast iron, adjustable... unbreakable."

He stared at it for a while, running his fingers along the timber. "It's indestructible, right?"

"Sturdy as hell," I answered.

Without another word, Cooper simply disappeared down the hall, only to return with a bottle of lube and a condom. He put them on the edge of the dining table near the drafting board and looked over at me with mischief in his eyes, then he stretched up slowly and grabbed the top of the board.

"You're ambitious," I told him. "It's that Gen Y thing that gets you into trouble."

He spread his legs and lifted his ass. His voice was gruff. "It's a horny thing. But I didn't offer myself in my fantasy. You... *took* me."

I walked over to him and pressed him against the drafting board. "Like this?"

He moaned his response, so I reached around him and undid his belt and pants, sliding them over his hips. Then I undid mine. I rubbed my naked cock along the crack of his ass, smeared us both with lube, then when he heard the tear of the foil packet, he lifted his leg onto the bottom wooden brace.

"Please."

When I pushed into him, I slid my hands up his arms to the top of the drafting board and gripped my hands over his. And I fucked him. Just like he wanted me to. Just like how he groaned, begging me, pleading with me.

Afterward, when we'd collapsed into a sticky, sated mess on the sofa, I said, "So, you really like the new drafting board?"

He looked at me and waggled his eyebrows. "Yeah, I happen to love antiques."

I narrowed my eyes at him, knowing he meant me, and he burst out laughing.

"You're such a little shit."

"You love me."

I deliberately didn't say anything, so he dug his fingers into my ribs. "Say it! Say it," he said, laughing.

"Yes, I do," I barked out with a laugh. "I *do* love you."

He grinned victoriously, so I added, "You little shit."

ON SATURDAY MORNING, we'd checked our luggage in at the airport and sat down for coffee before our boarding call when Cooper pulled out his cell. He scrolled for a number and pressed call.

"Mom?" he asked. "Yeah, we're just at LaGuardia now." I could hear his mother saying something, then Cooper smiled. "Yes, Tom's here with me," he said. "Actually, Mom, you've met him before."

I put my coffee down.

"Yes, you have," Cooper told her. "Remember my friend from high school, Ryan Elkin?" Then he added ever so calmly, "Well, Tom's his dad."

There was silence for a moment, and Cooper looked at me unapologetically. "No, I'm not joking... Yes, because I want you to meet him..." He was quiet then while his mother obviously spoke. I could hear her voice through the phone.

"No," he said with less of a smile. "We've rented a car. We'll just see you at your place"—he looked at his watch—"in about three hours."

He clicked off the call and I asked him, "Couldn't wait to tell her?"

He shrugged and sighed. "Now she has three hours to get used to the idea before we walk in the front door."

I sipped my coffee. "True," I conceded. "But over the phone?"

"I know my mother," he said. "Three hours. First hour, she'll be livid with me for dropping that bombshell. Second hour, she'll be mad because, well, you're older than my dad, and by the third hour she'll have had enough time to calm down."

I laughed at his blasé comment. "'She'll be mad because, well, you're older than my dad,'" I repeated, shaking my head. "Jeez, Coop. Thanks."

He chuckled. "Don't sweat it, babe. She'll be fine with it... when she gets used to it."

"Don't sweat it, babe?" I echoed. "Is that some Gen Y thing for 'it'll be fine'?"

"Yes," he said seriously. "You should take notes, old man."

Ignoring that, I asked, "And your dad? How will he take it?"

Cooper put down his coffee and said, "I'm thinking not very well." He looked down at the table, and for the first time since I'd met him, he looked... uncertain.

"Cooper, I'll be there with you," I promised him. "If he... We'll be there together to talk to them."

A voice over the loudspeaker called our flight, and we boarded the plane. Cooper said he wasn't nervous, that he was okay, but the closer we got to Chicago, the tighter he held my hand.

CHAPTER NINE

COOPER WAS AMAZING. Yes, he was nervous, but after we'd collected the rental car, I asked him if he'd like to check in at the hotel first. He shook his head. "Nope, wanna get this out of the way."

That was Cooper. Jump in with both feet and tackle it head-on. One thing was for certain, when he made his mind up, there was no point trying to persuade him otherwise.

He was remarkable like that. Some might argue that he was more foolish than courageous, but at just twenty-two years of age, sometimes I thought he was light years ahead of me.

And then other times, he was a twenty-two-year-old fucking kid. Like driving, for instance. Claiming I didn't know where his parents lived, he took the car keys, then proceeded to drive, according to him, like he stole it.

Twenty minutes and fifteen old-man-with-a-heart-condition jokes later, he pulled the car into the drive of his parent's house. It was a large, two-story house surrounded by manicured lawns with well-kept flower beds. Cooper's parents had obviously done well for themselves since moving to Chicago.

Cooper exhaled through puffed cheeks and looked at me like 'here goes nothing,' opened the car door, and got out.

I followed him, and he waited for me to step up beside him at the front door before he rang the doorbell.

Meeting his parents was, for the lack of some profound, life-changing word, weird.

His mother, Paula, opened the door as if she were expecting some other, younger Tom, and Cooper's joke of dating Tom Elkin was just that. A joke.

When she saw me, she stared—just stared—before she even remembered to say hello to her son. She kissed his cheek. We walked in and met Cooper's father, Andrew, in the living room. I'd met them both, maybe once or twice, when Cooper and Ryan had been at school, and they hadn't changed one bit.

Cooper and I sat down on the sofa, his parents sat across from us, and still not a word was spoken.

Just awkward stares, coupled with awkward silences.

But then a kid walked in, who I realized must have been Max, Cooper's younger brother. He was seventeen years old and going through what Cooper called an 'emo' phase. He had longish black hair swept over half his face and there was a nose ring on the half I could see.

Max stopped when he saw Cooper, looked at me for a long second, then back to Cooper. "Dude," he said slowly. "He's old."

I looked at Cooper, Cooper looked at me, then both of us burst out laughing. Even his mother tried not to smile. His father, on the other hand, didn't look so impressed.

Cooper stood up and gave his little brother a bit of a

hug, then tried to touch the nose ring, but Max dodged him easily. "Nice silverware," Cooper said.

"Thanks," he replied.

Cooper roughed up his brother's hair. "Do the girls like it?"

Max pushed Cooper and tried to smack him upside his head. "Like you'd know."

"Boys," Paula chastised. "Cooper, you've been here for thirty seconds. Leave your brother alone."

Cooper walked over to where I was sitting and he sat down, a little closer to me this time. Max stood behind his parents, Cooper made a face at him, and Max flipped him the bird.

"Cooper," his father said. "Can you be serious for a moment? I think we have some... *issues* that need discussing."

Cooper took my hand. "Mom, Dad, this is Tom. Yes, he's older than me, but we're together, and we're serious."

His parents both stared at him, then turned their attention to me, and it was my turn to talk. "I know you're thinking this is wrong, or that it can't be real," I said calmly. "And believe me, I don't think we were expecting any of this either, but the fact we're both here must tell you we're serious."

"You're old enough to be his father," Paula whispered.

"Yes, I am," I answered.

"Age isn't an issue," Cooper said quickly. "Not for us. It's never been an issue." Then he said, "Well, in the beginning, it was a little weird. Before we got together and I was attracted to him, I kept thinking 'Oh my God, he's forty-four,' but then I realized it didn't matter."

I looked at him and squeezed his hand.

"It didn't matter?" his father asked.

"No, it wasn't his *age* that I was interested in," Cooper told them. "It was the fact we'd spend hours talking about anything and everything, like I'd met my intellectual match."

I couldn't help but smile, and his admission of exactly how I felt reinforced to me that this was worth it.

His father looked at the both of us like we didn't understand the obvious. "I'm sorry, Cooper, but it *does* matter."

Cooper's reply was a very serious, "Not to me."

Then his mother asked, "Just exactly how did this all come about?"

I retold the story, *sans* intimate details, of how we'd met, how we'd worked together, how it was then that I saw Cooper to be a person who was strong-minded, smart, and free-thinking.

Cooper's father glared at me. "You took *advantage* of him while he *worked* for you?"

I didn't have time to speak before Cooper sat forward on the sofa and spoke through gritted teeth. "He didn't take *advantage* of me!" He almost spat the words. "Jesus Christ!"

"Cooper, don't swear in this house," his mother chided.

Cooper ignored her. "So what you're saying is," he said, "you think I don't have a mind of my own, that I can't make my own decisions, and that I'm some easily led kid? Is that what you think?"

"No," his mother said, but his father stared at me.

They didn't think he was a naïve kid; they thought I was some sexual predator. I gave Cooper a small smile and squeezed his hand again. "It's not you they have a problem with."

"You think it's Tom?" he asked, looking at his parent's incredulously.

"I think a forty-four-year-old man should know better," his father replied.

"No," Cooper said flatly, dropping my hand to hold up both his index fingers. "No. Dad, you're not implying Tom should know better, you're implying I don't have the ability to see what's in front of me." He was angry, and his jaw bulged when he spoke. "Like I don't know what's right for me, like I'm some dumbass kid. Yes, Tom's a grown man, but you need to see that I am too."

"You're twenty-two years old," his father said. "And you're our son. We're allowed to be concerned. I don't think you have the perspective to see it for what it is, Cooper."

"I can't believe you have a problem with this." Cooper shook his head.

"I can't believe you thought we wouldn't have a problem with this," his father countered. "Quite frankly, Cooper, I can't see us ever not having a problem with this. I'm sorry, but I don't think it's right."

Cooper scratched his head, like he couldn't understand something. "You told me you'd accept me, all of me. You both said that. When I came out to you, when I finally admitted to you I was gay, you told me you'd love me no matter who I wanted or who I fell in love with."

Cooper stood up and walked to the back door, but then turned around. "But what you meant was that you'd only accept me if I fell in love with someone my own age. Or what? Someone that wasn't a guy?" he asked. "Oh God, were you still hoping me being gay was just a phase?" He was clearly upset. "Well, guess what? It's not a phase, and neither is this." He motioned between him and me. "I am *in love* with him."

His parents sat there, stunned at his outburst, and when they never said a word, Cooper turned on his heel and walked out of the door. I stood up, not excusing myself, not caring, and followed him.

He was walking across the yard to the pool. "Coop, sweetheart," I said, and he stopped and turned around. He had tears in his eyes.

"Can we go?" he asked. "I think I'd like to go now."

I put my hands around his neck and pulled him against me. "Sure," I told him. Not that I thought leaving was the best idea, but he needed me on his side right now.

He nodded against my neck. "I just want to go."

"Okay," I whispered.

"I thought they'd be okay," he mumbled. "I thought they'd be kinda mad, but then they'd see I was happy and they'd be okay."

"Maybe they need some time," I said. "They love you. They just want what's best for you."

"You're what's best for me," he answered, with his face still buried against me.

"Did you want to go?" I asked. "Or did you want to stay and try and sort this out?"

He sighed. "I want to go."

"Okay," I said again. "Whatever you want."

Cooper pulled back from me and took my hand. He led us into the house but never stopped. "Tell Max I said good-bye," he said to no one in particular and walked right past his parents to the front door.

I stopped him. "Just give me one minute," I said quietly.

He frowned and said, "I'll see you in the car." And not even looking at his mom or dad, he walked out.

I turned to face his parents. His father looked angry and confused, and his mother looked lost and utterly miserable. "He wants to leave," I told them. "He's very upset. Maybe it's not my place to say, and you can hate me all you like, but please don't lose him over this. Don't cut him off because of me."

"It won't be *our* doing," his father said coldly.

I smiled, despite the fact he was implying I would be the cause of Cooper losing his family. "I'm sure I don't have to tell you how stubborn Cooper is or how driven he is. Once he sets his sights on something, he stands his ground until he has it. By the same token, he won't stand for something he doesn't agree with, and he most certainly won't be walked over, and he won't be misled by anyone."

"What exactly are you saying?" Cooper's father asked.

I looked at them both. "That you raised an incredible son."

My words threw them, but eventually Paula asked, "What would you do? If it was your son? If it was Ryan who was dating someone twice his age."

I thought about that for a moment. "If he was happy, if it was what he wanted, then I'd tell him I loved him, knowing I'd be there for him if it fell apart."

Cooper's father scoffed. "Of course you would."

"All we can do is love them and hope they make the right choices," I said with my hand on the door handle. "Unconditional love is exactly that. We don't get to choose."

I opened the door wider, but before I left, I said, "We're staying at The Peninsula, on the eighteenth floor. Don't let him go back to New York thinking you don't love him."

I walked out to find Cooper in the passenger seat of the car instead of the driver's seat. I got in and pulled the car out onto the street and headed toward the city. Cooper was quiet and stared out the window for the trip to the hotel, and even after we'd checked in and went up to our suite, he was still silent.

He sat on the bed, and it was then he asked me what

had been said between his parents and me while he'd waited in the car, and I told him every word. His face fell and he frowned. "It wasn't supposed to go like that," he said.

It was heartbreaking to see him so upset. I pulled him against me and we lay back, and while he snuggled into me, I stared out over Chicago for I don't know how long.

When it started to get dark, I asked him if he wanted something to eat. "Or we can go out?" I suggested. "We can find whatever food you're in the mood for, or if you want to get drunk, we can do that too."

"Can we just stay in?" he asked. "I'm sorry, I'm not really in the mood to do anything."

"Don't apologize." I kissed his forehead. "Of course we can stay in. We can get room service."

"Sounds good."

"I can run you a bath. The hot tub is huge."

He finally smiled. "Maybe later."

I ordered us dinner, which he only picked at, and he declined the bath, opting for a hot shower, then he climbed into bed. I joined him, he slid into the crook of my arm, nestled into me, and fell asleep.

I lay there, staring at the ceiling, with an awful lot to think about.

I wondered if I should back off from Cooper, if I should urge him to choose his family over me. I certainly would never *make* him choose. But I had the perspective of both sides—as the boyfriend and as a father. It angered me that his parents wouldn't even consider the idea of Cooper and me being together. Maybe they were hoping I'd be the one to call it off with him, knowing, as a parent, I wouldn't want to be the cause of such a conflict.

And, well, that just pissed me off.

I wondered if this would change things between us. I

wondered, if his parents did give him an ultimatum, who he'd choose. As a parent, I wondered who I'd *want* him to choose.

I couldn't imagine leaving Cooper. I knew we'd only been together for a few months, but I loved him. I *adored* him—this incredible man who, for some reason, seemed to love me just as much as I loved him.

I wondered if he could leave me. I wondered if he should. And as that thought unsettled me, I tried to get out of bed, but Cooper's hold tightened on me. "Don't go," he mumbled.

I rolled so I faced him instead and wrapped him up in my arms. Even in his sleep, he needed me. How could I ever leave him? I hoped to God it wouldn't come to that. Instead, we could prove to them that we were serious. It wouldn't be easy, it would take patience and understanding, and it could very well take years.

But he was worth it. *We* were worth it.

I kissed the side of his head. "I'm not going anywhere."

IN THE MORNING, I woke up to find Cooper sitting on the bed with his phone in his hand. "Hey," I said, my voice still sleepy. "Everything okay?"

"Just got a message from Mom and Dad," he said, giving me a guarded smile. "They're coming to see us before we go back to New York."

CHAPTER TEN

IT WAS A VERY different meeting this time. Andrew and Paula Jones walked into the café at the hotel, looking more nervous than anything. Cooper's mother looked like she'd barely slept.

I knew how she felt.

Cooper was stoic, his jaw was set, and his chin was raised defiantly. I'd told him earlier, if he wanted to, he could listen to what they had to say, and if it didn't go well, the power was his to end the meeting.

If they didn't meet him halfway, at least.

He'd told me he'd hear them out, but he wouldn't put up with any bullshit about me coercing him into bed. He wouldn't cop being told he was just a kid or that I had no right to take advantage of him. He was hurt and angry, and I didn't blame him.

As tough as he tried to make himself out to be, he wanted their approval. He wanted his parents in his life, without any disagreements, without any tension. He wanted them to be happy for him.

Thankfully the waiter followed them in and took orders for coffee, which was an icebreaker for all of us.

His mother started first. "Cooper, honey, I'm sorry yesterday ended up the way it did I don't want to fight with you."

"I don't want to fight with you either," he said.

Then Paula stared at her husband, prompting him to speak.

"Look, son, we might not agree with everything you do," he said cautiously. He sighed and started again, "But it's not our choice. We know that."

I half expected him to say, 'it's not our mistake to make,' but thankfully, he didn't.

"No, it's not your choice," Cooper said. He wasn't letting them off easily. "It's my choice, and I've made it."

"We can see that," his mother said, trying to smile.

Just then, the waiter returned with coffee and asked if we were ready to order breakfast.

Cooper looked at his parents. "Will you be eating with us?" he asked. It wasn't really a question of food; it was a question of tolerance. If they stayed and ate with us, it meant they wanted to try to accept us.

"Yes," his mother said. "If that's okay with you?"

Cooper looked at his very quiet father. "Dad?"

"Yes," he said, clearing his throat. He looked to the waiter. "We're ready to order."

Cooper smiled and finally exhaled. He looked at me. "I'm starving. What are you having?"

It was hard not to smile back at him, even with his death-grip on my hand under the table. "Eggs Benedict, I think."

Cooper looked up at the waiter. "Pancakes with maple

syrup *and* bacon, and eggs Benedict, with ham, not salmon, sauce on the side, thanks."

The fact he ordered for me, knowing exactly how I liked my eggs done made me smile. It wasn't lost on his parents either.

It was pretty clear it was Paula who had insisted on this visit. His father was still standoffish, obviously not pleased with the idea of his son dating an older guy. But they were making an effort.

"Where's Max?" Cooper asked.

"Still in bed," Paula replied.

"He won't surface until lunchtime," his father mumbled.

Cooper looked up thoughtfully and sighed. "Ah, the good old days."

His mother smiled at him. "You should invite him to New York for a weekend," she said. "He'd love that."

"That'd be great," Cooper said. "I'm pretty busy with work, but we could line it up with a concert or something he wants to see." He looked at me and smiled. "Max loves thrash death-metal."

"Oh, excellent," I said sarcastically. "Another concert."

Cooper laughed. "You went to *one*, and you liked it."

"You went to one of his concerts?" Paula asked, surprised.

Cooper answered for me. "Of course he did. He takes me to those boring art exhibition openings, so it's only fair."

"You went to *one*," I countered, trying not to smile. "And you liked it."

Paula and Andrew looked on, not very sure what to make of our banter. Cooper smiled as he sipped his coffee. "You guys should come to New York," he said to his parents. "We could spend the weekend, I could show you where I work, we could go to Broadway or something equally as boring."

They agreed but didn't commit to anything, and conversation turned to Cooper's work, a subject he could talk about for hours. I just loved his enthusiasm for what he did, for what *we* did. He asked me a question or two, trying to drag me into the discussion, but I was happy for him to have this time with his parents. It didn't have to involve me at every turn.

I wanted them to see he was still the same person.

I answered him, of course, but let him take center stage. Not that I minded. I could listen to him talk about architecture all day long.

Cooper's parents might have caught me smiling at him a few times, but I didn't care. Let them see how much I admired him. I wasn't about to deny it.

Breakfast arrived, and as we ate, Paula directed her questions at me. She asked about my work, how I found New York, and she even made small talk about the Yankees.

But Andrew barely said a word.

When it was time to go, I told Cooper I'd give him a few minutes with his parents while I checked us out of the hotel and organized the car. When I couldn't put it off any longer, I met them in the lobby.

Cooper gave me a tight smile and quickly took my hand. After we'd said goodbye and were in the car on our way to the airport, I asked him what was said in my absence.

"Well, they're still not exactly happy about us," he answered.

"I'm sorry.".

"Don't you apologize," he said quickly. "For anything."

"Still, I'm sorry it didn't go how you'd hoped."

"Well," he said with a shrug, "they're prepared to put

up with it, so I guess that's all I could hope for." He looked at me as I drove, and gave me a sad smile. "Last night, I really thought they weren't going to accept it at all, so I guess *tolerance* is good."

"Coop, sweetheart, they're still a part of your life," I said. "They're talking of coming to New York to visit you. They might not 'accept' us being together, but they're trying. Give them time."

"I just wish they could see us, ya know?" he said, slowly shaking his head. "If they could see us, the way we are together, the way we talk and laugh..."

"I think they saw how happy you were, how serious we were," I told him, "and I think that's what scared them."

"Why would it scare them?" he asked. "Shouldn't they be happy for me?"

"Give them time," I said again. "I know it's a Gen Y thing to want everything yesterday, but some things take time."

He sighed and was quiet for a little while. Then he looked at me curiously. "What generation are you anyway?" he asked.

"Generation X," I answered.

"You had to Google that, didn't you?"

"Yes," I admitted with a laugh.

"So if I'm Gen Y and you're X, then together we are the chromosome code for male," he mused.

"Yes, I am X marks the spot, and you are the dear God, why, why, why."

"Fucking hell, Tom," he deadpanned. "We need to work on your jokes."

COOPER and I got back to New York and slipped easily back into our routine. He was busy with work, and it was something I understood well. I actually condoned it. If he wanted to be the best—and he could be with his talent—he needed to put in the hours.

It was what I'd done. It was what had gotten me where I was today.

So if he had to work late, I didn't mind. If he brought work over to my place, I did my work alongside him.

It was what we did.

We worked, we talked, we laughed, we made out, then we worked some more. He didn't stay over every night that week, but almost. "It really would be easier if you moved in here," I told him.

Cooper was standing near the dining table, packing some papers into his messenger bag. He dropped his hand. "Really, Tom?" he asked, not too happily. "*Easier?* It'd be *easier?*"

"Well, it's a pain you always having to come here or me going to your place," I said, but my words lost steam with the look on his face. "Easier was the wrong word, wasn't it?"

He nodded. "Yeah, it really was."

"I'm sorry."

Cooper finished stuffing his belongings into his bag and walked over to me, kissing me with smiling lips. "You keep getting the whole move-in-with-me speech wrong."

"Can I try again?"

"Not tonight."

Damn, he was a demanding little punk. "Let me call you a cab."

"I can call my own cab," he said with a smile. "Well, Lionel will call one for me."

"Lionel hails you a cab?"

"Yep," he answered with a grin. "I told you he loves me."

"Did you bring him a jar of peanut butter?" I asked with a smirk. "Did you *flatter* him the way you *flattered* me?"

"No, I bought him struffoli from the Italian bakery on East Fifty-Third," he said simply. "Well, technically I bought them for his wife who's from Naples, so he was in her good books, and I'm in his."

"I can't believe you did that." I shook my head. "Wait. Wait, you gave him fine Italian pastries and all I got was peanut butter?"

Cooper laughed. "I bought you peanut butter because I wanted a sandwich. The coffee was to win you over."

"You're unbelievable."

"I know," he answered simply. "Coffee and sass. I bought you coffee and sass."

I chuckled as he got to the door. "Cooper?"

"Yeah?"

"I'm glad you bought me coffee."

He grinned and walked out. I heard him yell from the hall. "And sass."

I nodded and grinned to myself. "And sass."

I SPOKE to Cooper every day on the phone or via text but didn't see him for the rest of the week.

I missed him.

So on Friday night when I was supposed to be meeting some business friends of mine, I called and asked Cooper if he'd like to come.

"They're your friends," he said. "They've known you for twenty years. Is that a good idea?"

"Of course it is," I told him. "I want them to meet you."

I heard him switch his phone to his other ear. "But it's Chaney, Hilderbrandt, and Myer."

"So?"

"Jesus, Tom," he whispered into the phone. "They're like the holy trinity of architecture."

I laughed. "Really, Cooper? They're just friends of mine."

"'They're just friends of mine,'" he repeated sarcastically. "God, I keep forgetting you're in the same league as them."

"Thanks," I scoffed.

"You know what I mean," he tried to explain. "I studied their work in college. They're like legends."

"Did you study *my* work in college?"

"Enough of the ego, Elkin."

I laughed into the phone. "You *did* study my work!" I cried, but all he did was mumble some noncommittal response. I took a deep breath and tried not to smile. "Will you please come to dinner with me?" I asked. Then I whispered, "I've missed you."

"Okay," he relented petulantly. "I'll be nervous and probably say something to embarrass you and they'll laugh at me and I'll never work in the industry again, but I'll go because you asked."

"You'll be fine," I told him. "Just be yourself. They'll love you."

———

WELL, he was a little late, but that gave me enough time to tell the three men I met there I was expecting my date.

My boyfriend.

They'd known I'd split from Sofia, although I hadn't really found the courage to tell them the real reason until almost a year after. The three of them were what Cooper would call *old school*, but they were also my friends. They'd said they didn't care that I was gay, and I'd met with them many times since, and things between us were the same as they'd always been. Granted, I'd also never brought a date.

The restaurant was on Madison and Fifth, fine dining and strict dress code. I wondered briefly if I should have elaborated that fact to Cooper earlier, but when he walked in, he was still wearing his suit.

I stood when the maître D' escorted him over and gave him a reassuring smile. He was nervous. "Sorry I'm late," he said quietly. "Louisa has me working on the Philly project."

Cooper took off his jacket, revealing his charcoal waistcoat and gray shirt and tie, and looked expectantly, nervously, around the table. I made introductions, and Cooper smiled and said polite hellos. I'd never seen him so anxious. I didn't want anyone to be uncomfortable with public displays of affection, Cooper included, but I wanted to reassure him. So under the table, I slid my foot alongside Cooper's, silently telling him I was there. He gave me a small, appreciative smile.

Hal Meyers spoke first. "Tom says you're working with Louisa Arlington?"

"Yes," Cooper said. "She's great. I'm working on a project at the moment that we're taking to the Green Exhibition in Philly next week. It's amazing."

And so conversation turned to architecture, but with five architects at the table, it was inevitable. I kind of hoped it would, knowing it was a safe topic of conversation for Cooper. And I also wanted them to see how switched on he was.

He was quiet at first, but as conversation opened up, he spoke animatedly, reining himself in every now and then. I think the others asked him questions to test him, but he spoke about new design concepts, and how airflow principals and insulation should co-exist to reduce energy output and how sustainability was the responsibility of his generation of designers.

I was sure Cooper would start on a tangent, then remind himself just who he was sitting at the table with. Whether it was his nerves or his blatant love for what he did, I wasn't sure.

After we'd eaten and when he'd excused himself to go to the bathroom, the three men watched him leave. Lloyd Chaney raised his eyebrows. "He's certainly on his way in the world, isn't he?"

"Yes," I agreed. "He's very passionate about what he does."

"He's very young," Ro Hilderbrandt said. He wasn't talking about Cooper's age for his profession. He was talking about his relationship with me.

"He is," I conceded. "But I assure you, he has twice the talent than what any of us did when we were his age."

"Are you hoping he'll tutor you?" Hal joked.

"I shouldn't laugh," I said with a smile. "Because I promise you, new design principles will leave us old fogeys for dead. He probably could teach me a thing or two about where our industry's going."

"Old fogeys?" Ro scoffed. "We're not that old. You might feel it because you've scored yourself someone half your age."

I ignored his jibe. "He's really nervous about being here tonight."

Lloyd turned his wine glass in his fingertips. "You must be serious about him if you've brought him to meet us."

I sighed. "Yes."

"How did you meet?" Hal asked.

"He's a friend of Ryan's," I said, deliberately not telling them about Cooper's internship. It was a discussion I didn't want to have, knowing Cooper would be back any second, so I changed the subject. "When I told him who we'd be having dinner with tonight, he called you three the holy trinity of architecture."

Cooper came back to his seat, as the three of them were still chuckling, and looked at me nervously. "I just told them how they'd be known as the holy trinity of architecture from now on."

Cooper groaned. "Yeah, thanks. I was going to make the *Godfather* analogy but figured I didn't want to give you ideas about young architects offending his mentors," he said, looking at me pointedly. "Besides, I hear horse heads are hard to come by this time of year."

Ro, Hal, and Lloyd all laughed at his joke, and I slipped my hand on Cooper's leg under the table.

Hal said, "Well, if we're the holy trinity, what's the great Thomas Elkin?"

Cooper looked at me and shrugged. "He's just Tom."

They all laughed again, but Ro laughed the loudest. "That's the first time I've ever heard Thomas Elkin be called 'just Tom,'" he said.

Lloyd nodded. "I like you, son," he said to Cooper. "It's about time Tom here had some ego checks."

Cooper looked to the table, a little embarrassed, so I gave his leg a squeeze. "Gentlemen, on that note, before I'm the punch line to any more of your jokes, we'll bid you goodnight." I knew they meant no harm. It was just how they were.

"Yes, I must be getting home too," Hal said. "Sue's had one of her book-club meetings, but I think it'll be safe to go home by now."

We paid our bill and walked out, shook hands, and agreed we'd do it again in another month or so, like we always did.

Cooper was quiet on the way back to my apartment. I asked him if he wanted to go home, but he held my hand tighter and said no. When we finally got inside, he was frowning. "Did I say something wrong?"

I walked around to where he was leaning his ass on the dining table. I put my hands on his face and made him look at me. "Cooper Jones, you were perfect tonight," I whispered. "Their jibes at me were nothing to do with you. It's how we are when we all get together. They're old country-club-style, men's-club boys. They're always like that. Actually," I said, "I think they took us pretty well, all things considered."

Cooper nodded but didn't seem convinced. "I just felt stupid."

"You're *not* stupid. You're far from stupid," I said seriously. "They said to me when you'd gone to the bathroom how switched on you were."

He looked at me with imploring eyes. "Really?"

"Ready to take on the world."

"I called you 'just Tom.'"

I nodded and pecked his lips. "So? I like being just Tom."

He gave me a half-smile. "You're *my* just Tom."

"Yes, I am," I whispered before I kissed him again.

———————————

CHAPTER ELEVEN

COOPER WORKED most of the weekend. He spent the day with his head in books, looking at the laptop screen or scribbling down notes.

I didn't mind.

I lounged on the sofa for a while, read the papers, made him coffee, nuzzled his neck, made him lunch, made him laugh, then annoyed him some more.

Eventually, realizing I wasn't going to deter him, I pulled out my own work, cleared some room on the dining table, and joined him. We had a lazy dinner, I gave him some stress relief in bed by lavishing his entire body with my mouth, and we fell asleep wrapped around each other.

Sunday was much the same. It was a perfect way to spend the weekend. Well, it was for me, but Cooper was looking a little stressed. He was sitting at the dining table and had just run his hand through his hair for about the twentieth time.

"I just want this to be perfect," he said when I asked him what was wrong. "It's my first big project, and Louisa trusts me with it. I know it's not my project alone, but I need to make sure what I contribute is perfect."

I kissed the top of his head. "Don't underestimate yourself," I told him. "Everything you do is perfect."

He looked up at me and grinned. "Everything?"

"Mm-hmm," I hummed. "Some things a little more perfect than others, but yes."

"Excuse me, Mr. Elkin, do I hear a sexual innuendo in your tone?"

"There's quite the possibility you do, Mr. Jones," I said with a smirk.

Cooper stood up from the dining chair and kissed me. "No innuendos for you, Mr. Elkin. I need to get home."

I raised my eyebrows. It was the first time ever he'd not been interested in sex. "You know, I think that's a first."

He smiled. "I have laundry to do, and I need to get organized for tomorrow."

"You're passing me over to do laundry?"

He laughed, but then he groaned. "Aw, that's not fair."

I smiled and kissed him. "Seriously, Cooper, I don't mind. I'm just joking."

"I'll make it up to you during the week."

I sighed dramatically. "You know, if you lived here..."

He narrowed his eyes at me. "You want sex that bad?"

I barked out a laugh. "No!"

"Then what?"

"Well, I have a laundry service—" I stopped midsentence from the look on his face.

"So, I should move in for sex and free laundry?"

"No!"

"That is the worst move-in-with-me speech ever," he said. "In the history of the world."

I was gaping but smiling and shaking my head. "No,

that's not what I was saying at all."

Cooper shook his head then clicked his tongue. "Tsk, tsk." Then he sighed dramatically. He was trying not to smile. "That was your worst one yet."

My head fell back and I groaned. "Cooper Jones, you're infuriating and unreasonable, and *you* made it all about sex and laundry."

He laughed. "Infuriating and unreasonable? Jeez, this just gets better. Remember when I used to be cute?"

I grabbed his chin between my thumb and forefinger and kissed him. "Have fun doing your laundry."

"I will," he said cheerfully. "And I'll see you on Wednesday after work." He packed up his papers, his laptop, and threw it all in his satchel, and we walked to the front door.

I leaned against the jamb and stopped him from leaving. "You're still cute. You're still infuriating and unreasonable. But you're addictive and you're wonderful."

He stepped up close and kissed me softly. "I love you too, Tom."

I smiled and rested my forehead on his. "One day you'll agree to move in, and you won't have to keep leaving," I said quietly. "And my place wouldn't feel so empty."

A slow smile spread across his face and he sighed. "Mmm, almost. Not quite, but that's the best by far."

"I wasn't trying to ask you to move in."

He kissed me sweetly again. "Maybe that's why." With that, he walked out and down the hall, smiling as he looked back at me.

"Did I mention infuriating?" I asked.

He pressed the elevator button. "Good night, Tom."

"Maddening?"

The elevator doors opened, and he smiled. "I'll call

you later."

"Exasperating?"

"Love you," he called out as the doors were closing.

"Love you too," I called back. "You little shit."

"Heard that," he said quickly, but the elevator closed, then he was gone.

I shut the door, and when I looked around my apartment to see his mess strewn all over it, I smiled.

I'D SPOKEN to Cooper on the phone several times over the next few days, and he'd said he would be over at my place on Wednesday after work. He'd thought it'd be about seven by the time he finished up for the day, so I was surprised to hear his keys in the front door barely after six.

I walked around from the kitchen just as he was coming through the door. "Hey you," I said. "You're early. Everything okay?"

Cooper nodded as he dumped his messenger bag on the floor. He walked directly up to me and smiled. "I missed you," he said, then he kissed me. Hard. And he pushed me backward toward the hall, toward my bedroom. He broke the kiss to say, "I shouldn't have said no to sex on Sunday."

I laughed as I pulled his shirt up and loosened his tie. "Tell me what you want."

"I want it all," he murmured, trying to kiss my neck while undoing his pants. "I want you to do everything to me."

"Everything?"

Cooper then fumbled with my fly until he could slip his hand in and wrap his hand around me. "Everything."

By the time we were naked on the bed, and by the time

I had made him come the first time, he was begging me. I kissed him, licked him, and sucked him. I rimmed him, fingered him, then I fucked him.

He wanted everything. So that was what I did to him.

Afterwards, when he'd come the second time, I discarded the condom and lay back beside him. He looked at me with glazed-over eyes and he chuckled. "Jesus," he said, still catching his breath.

"You said everything."

He laughed again, just as his cell phone rang. With a groan, he rolled to the end of the bed and almost fell off trying to get his phone from his pants pocket. He was still laughing when he answered. "Yes, Louisa?"

He was quiet while his boss spoke to him, but he was still naked in my bed, so I commando-crawled over to him, licking his spent cock, seeing if there was a third time in him.

He squirmed and pushed me back, somehow rolling on top of me, still with his phone to his ear. "Louisa, I don't think I can," he said seriously. His eyes flickered between mine. "I have plans... well, they're important plans."

Then he climbed off me, sat cross-legged on my bed, still naked. "Louisa, Tom and I are going to see his parents," he said. "It's kind of important..." He ran his hand through his hair. "Well, actually, he's right here... Okay," he said slowly. "I'll put him on." Cooper frowned and held out his phone. "Louisa needs me to work this weekend."

I took the phone. "Hello, Louisa, it's Tom."

"Oh, Tom," she said into the phone. "How are you? Cooper talks about you all the time."

"I'm really well," I answered. I looked at the man in my bed. "Never better, actually. How are you? It's been a while."

"I'm great," she said. "I've been meaning to call you and thank you for recommending Cooper. He's really taken strides since he started."

"Yes, he has."

"Cooper says you have a family commitment this weekend," she said.

"We had plans, yes," I explained. "We were heading up to see my parents."

"You know we have the Philadelphia exhibition coming up."

"Louisa, I can't tell him what to do or make decisions on his behalf. I did that once and he tore shreds off me. But I can *suggest* to him, in my professional opinion, that it'd be in *his* professional interest to work. We can see my parents another time."

Cooper shook his head. "We said we'd go," he whispered.

Louisa said, "Tore shreds off you, did he?" I could hear the smile in her voice.

"Yes, it wasn't pretty."

She laughed. "He's a strong-minded one, isn't he?"

"You have no idea," I said with a smile.

Cooper snatched the phone from me and rolled his eyes.

"Louisa, can I call you back?" he asked. "Five minutes."

He threw his phone beside us on the bed and took my hand. "Tom, we agreed we'd go and see your parents."

"And your Philly exhibition is extremely important."

"So are you. So is telling your parents."

I squeezed his hand and smiled. "Coop, sweetheart, we can go another weekend to see my parents. The date of your first exhibition can't change."

He sighed. "I don't want you to think—"

"I understand. I truly do." I lifted his hand to my lips and kissed his knuckles. "You've worked so hard on this job, you need to go."

He frowned and sighed again. "What will you do?"

I smiled at his concern that I couldn't possibly survive a weekend without him. "There's no reason why I can't go see my parents anyway," I told him. "I haven't spent much time with them lately, aside from the occasional phone call. It'll be nice."

He was quiet for a long few seconds. "Will you tell them?"

"I don't know," I answered honestly. "I'll test the waters first. I want to tell them. I need to tell them. I'd kind of psyched myself up for it to be this weekend, but I know I said we'd do it together."

"I want to be there for you," he said quietly. "In case... well, in case it doesn't go well."

"I'm a big boy," I said with a smile. "I love that you want to be there. But if I get there and the timing is right, I'll tell them. I want to tell them about you, that I finally met someone who understands me. It's not the 'oh, by the way, I'm gay' speech I want to tell them, it's that I met you. *That's* what I want to tell them."

He smiled shyly for me. "Maybe giving them some warning might be a good idea," he said. "Before we go up together."

"And you need to kick ass in Philly."

"I don't exactly have that much to do there," he said with a shrug.

"Louisa wants you to see the whole process," I presumed. "It'll be good experience for you."

He turned my hand over in his and pouted. "Will you miss me?"

I lay back on the bed and laughed. "Every minute."

"Just every minute?"

I reached over, picked up his phone, and tossed it to him. "Call Louisa. I'll figure out dinner."

I pulled on a pair of jeans and left him to make the call. After I'd ordered some takeout, I grabbed two beers from the fridge just as Cooper walked out. He was wearing a pair of my sleep pants.

I looked him up and down. "Not wearing those home, I hope."

"Not going home tonight."

I handed him a beer and kissed him lightly on the lips. "When do you leave for Philly?"

"First thing Saturday morning," he said. "So I might have to stay here Friday night as well."

I grinned. "I think you might."

———

I OFFERED to drive Cooper to the airport to save him the cab fare, so as a trade-off, he went for two takeaway coffees while I finished getting ready.

I told him I'd bring our overnight bags down to the car, and when I got to the lobby, Cooper was walking back in with three coffees in a cardboard tray. He handed one to Lionel, who at first refused the offer, but then took it at Cooper's insistence.

I put the overnight bag and Cooper's messenger bag down, and Lionel jumped with a start. "Oh, let me get those for you, Mr. Elkin," he said quickly. He looked at the coffee he was holding, not sure where to put it.

"It's fine, Lionel," I said with a smile. "We're heading down to the parking lot."

"Are you heading out of town?" Lionel asked. "How long can I expect you gone?"

"Just overnight," Cooper answered. "I'm leaving first, then Tom will go before lunch, in different directions this time. Not sure how Tom will cope without me."

I rolled my eyes and took my coffee from him. "You can carry your own bags."

Cooper feigned offense. "Hey, I thought the elderly revered chivalry."

I looked at Lionel. "See what I have to put up with?"

Cooper nudged poor Lionel with his elbow. "And he absolutely wouldn't have it any other way."

Lionel hid his smile behind his coffee cup. "Well, I hope you both have an enjoyable weekend, even if it's in different directions."

Cooper walked over toward his bags and said, "Lionel, tell Mrs. Lionel I said hello. If she needs anymore of that struffoli any time soon, you just let me know."

"Will do, Mr. Jones," Lionel said with a nod. "Thank you very much."

I shook my head at him and his ability to charm anyone. "You ready?"

He nodded and smiled handsomely. Then he picked up his overnight bag and held it out for me to carry. He batted his eyelids, and with a sigh and dramatic eye roll, I took it with my free hand. He picked up his satchel, looked back at Lionel and grinned.

"You're such a little shit," I mumbled.

"It's a Gen-Y thing," he said cheerfully.

"It's a Cooper-Jones thing." Then I added, "It's a pain in the ass thing."

"You love the pain in your ass thing."

Knowing I would never win, I chose to give up on that

line of conversation and pressed the elevator button to go to the parking lot instead. And as we got into the car and headed out into New York traffic, Cooper said, "You know, Mr. and Mrs. Lionel don't have kids."

"Mr. and Mrs. Lionel?" I asked. "You do know that's his first name?"

Cooper nodded. "Yeah, but I don't know his last name or his wife's first name, so I call them Mr. and Mrs. Lionel."

"Yet you know she likes struffoli?"

He smiled proudly. "Of course. It's all in the questions."

"Apparently you ask the wrong ones."

"Or the right ones," he said with a smirk. "Anyway, as I was saying, they don't have kids." Then he added thoughtfully, "I think they might want to adopt me."

I laughed at him. "You're incorrigible."

He smiled as though I'd complimented him. "It's a talent."

"It's one of your finest."

Cooper grinned at me. "So, are you going to see me off at the airport? Stand in the terminal lounge, staring out the window, waiting for my plane to take off?"

I snorted. "Um, no. I was going to drop you off at the departure terminal so I didn't have to get a parking spot."

He gaped and narrowed his eyes. "When you get home, do me a favor and Google the word chivalry," he said flatly. "It's spelled *c-h-i-v—*"

"Shut up," I said with a laugh.

"Or even look up the definition of 'nice boyfriend.' I'm pretty sure it says 'does not drop off loved one at terminal gate' or 'does not tell boyfriend to shut up.'"

I laughed at him, but he smiled smugly when I turned into the ludicrously expensive parking lot instead of pulling up at the terminal doors. I even carried his bag *and* his messenger bag to the check-in counter.

"See, I know what chivalry means," I told him.

Cooper hooked his arm through mine. "And you do it well."

"Do I really have to wait until your plane leaves?"

"Maybe just until I board."

"Even that long?"

"Your chivalry is starting to wane."

"It comes and goes."

He rolled his eyes dramatically. "Oh, just like you. You came this morning, and now you want to go."

I barked out a laugh. "Okay, you win. I'll buy you another coffee."

"And a croissant."

I led him to a coffee shop in the terminal, and it wasn't until he was about to board his plane that he was serious. "If you want to tell your parents today, then tell them. Do what feels right," he said. "If you think it won't go well, you can wait and we'll tell them together."

I pulled him in for a hug and kissed the side of his neck. "Thank you, Cooper. You have a good time down in Philly. Show them what you can do."

He sighed against me. "Call me if you need to talk," he said. "About anything."

"You'll be so busy," I told him, pulling back so I could see his face. "How about you call me when you get to your hotel tonight? It doesn't matter what time."

"Okay," he agreed.

I knew exactly what he was about to say. "Don't apologize. Last time you saw my parents, at Ryan's birthday, you had to pretend we weren't together. The next time you see them, I want them to know exactly who you are."

"Oh, they'll love me," he said casually. "Everybody does. I'm more worried how they'll be with you."

I rolled my eyes and sighed loudly. "Go get on your plane. Before you take off, do me a favor and Google the word 'cranter.'"

I could tell by the look on his face he didn't know what the word meant. I smiled and kissed him lightly. "Bye."

I hadn't even driven out of the parking lot before my phone beeped with a message.

Your use of the Urban Dictionary is outstanding, smartass.

When I pulled up at traffic lights, I typed out my response. *Your proper nouns could use some work.*

From chivalry to insolent in twenty minutes.

I replied with his earlier comment to me. *It's a talent.*

I'm putting on my earphones and ignoring your insolent, gorgeous smartass.

I smiled as I typed out my response. *I love you too.*

I SMILED ALL the way home, packed my bag, and by the time I'd driven up the coast to my mom and dad's house, I was even more determined to tell them.

I wanted them to know about the person who challenged me, who drove me crazy, who made me laugh. Who loved me.

I wanted them to know. I knew they wouldn't take the news very well, but Cooper was worth it.

The closer I got to my parents' house, the more determined I was. But as I pulled into their street, everything changed. Because there were blue-and-red flashing lights and an ambulance in their driveway.

CHAPTER TWELVE

I PULLED up and raced out of the car to the back of the ambulance. My father was lying on the gurney, with an oxygen mask on his face marred by pale puffs of breath. He looked asleep as they loaded him in the back of the vehicle.

Despite my father obviously being ill, I knew things really weren't good from the look on my mother's face. Her soft, usually ever-smiling face was now etched with worry and stained with tears. There was a female paramedic standing beside her.

"Mom, what's wrong?" I asked, almost running to her. "What happened to Dad?"

Her eyes darted to Dad, then the paramedic gave me a sad smile. "You're Tom?" the woman asked. "Your mother said you'd be here soon."

"Yes," I answered. "Can you tell me what's going on? What's wrong with my father?"

"Your father has suffered what we suspect is a massive stroke," she answered. "We're taking him to the hospital."

"Okay," I said rather stupidly, trying to process everything. "Which one?"

"South Hampton," the paramedic said, and she moved to the back of the ambulance.

Another paramedic got out from the back of the ambulance and slipped into the driver's side. She looked pointedly at Mom. "We need to go."

"Mom, you go with Dad in the ambulance." I ushered her toward the van.

She seemed unable to move.

"I'll lock the house up and meet you there. You go."

Mom blinked a few times. The paramedic kindly helped her into the back of the ambulance, the lights started to flash, and they left.

And I stood there, staring at where they'd just been.

That wasn't how it was supposed to go at all.

I stood, lost, stuck until my mind finally told my body to move. I ran inside, closed and locked windows and doors, grabbed my mother's handbag and keys, and locked the front door behind me.

I don't remember the drive to the hospital.

When I got to the emergency room, after telling them who I was there to see, I was ushered through the double doors and found my mother, sitting, waiting, alone. "They're working on him now," she said quietly. "He had another stroke in the ambulance."

Fuck.

I took her hand and held it as tight as I dared.

"He said he was feeling funny this morning," she whispered. "Said he thought he should have a nap. I took a cup of tea in to him not long after," she said, starting to cry. "But he couldn't move. He just stared at me."

I pulled my mom against me and held her while she sobbed quietly in my arms. And then a man in scrubs walked out to stand in front of us. "Mrs. Elkin," he said.

"We're taking your husband in for surgery. He's had scans. There's considerable swelling on his brain and a blockage. We'll do everything we can..." His words trailed off.

"But?" I asked.

"But it doesn't look good," he replied gently.

My blood ran cold and my stomach knotted. I squeezed my mom's hand.

"If there's any other family you need to call...," he suggested, then turned and walked down the hall.

I let his words sink in for a long moment before I took my phone from my pocket. I scrolled through my contacts and hit call.

He picked up on the third ring. "Dad?"

"Yeah, Ryan, it's me," I said softly.

———

IT WAS A LONG, anxious wait sitting beside Mom in the waiting room, waiting for word, waiting for anything.

I was hoping Ryan would get there before the doctors came out to speak to us, but it didn't work out that way.

The same doctor as before walked out, and I knew from the look on his face that the news wasn't good. He looked at me first, then to Mom, and he frowned. "I'm sorry," he started. "Your husband suffered a heart attack, and with the blockage in the brain... We did everything we could."

Mom's hand went to her mouth and she started to cry, saying, "No, no, no," over and over. The doctor offered quiet condolences, and as he left, Mom surprised me and stood up. "I want to see him."

The doctor looked at me, then back to the heartbroken woman in front of him. "Come with me," he said gently.

They disappeared through the doors he'd just come through, and again, I was left not knowing what to do.

My father was gone.

Forever.

He was only sixty-seven.

I heard a familiar voice and turned to see Ryan come down the hall. He was almost running, and his mother was behind him. Sofia must have driven him here. "Dad?" Ryan asked. "How is he?"

I stood up, and I was pretty sure I didn't have to say. The look on my face must have said enough. I shook my head and said the hardest words I'd ever said to him. "He's gone."

Ryan's whole body sagged. "He what?"

"Your grandfather's gone," I said again. "It was a massive stroke."

Ryan shook his head and looked disbelievingly from me to Sofia. His eyes welled with tears. "No."

I put my arms around him and held him while he cried. I looked at Sofia, who had fresh tears running down her cheeks. "Thank you for bringing him," I said softly. "Thank you."

She put her hand on my shoulder. "Are you okay, Tom?"

"I'll be fine," I answered, nodding weakly. I *had* to be fine. I needed to be strong. My mother and my son needed me, and I had to be the strong one. I pulled back from Ryan and let him wipe his eyes with the back of his hands.

"Mom's just gone with the doctor," I told them, as we sat down in the waiting room chairs. "She wanted to see him before... She wanted to see him."

Ryan nodded. "Where's Cooper?"

"He's in Philadelphia," I told him in a whisper. "He left

this morning for the green energy convention he's been working on."

Ryan wiped at his nose and nodded. "That's right. I forgot." Then he said, "What do we do now? With Grandpa? And Grandma? What happens?"

"I don't know," I answered honestly. "I'll see what Mom wants to do. I might suggest she come home with me, but knowing her, she'll want to go home."

"If you need me to do anything," Sofia said softly, "please, just ask."

I gave her a nod. Sofia always loved my parents, and they loved her, so it really wasn't surprising that she'd offered to help. It wasn't surprising that she was here. She would take the loss of my father similar to the loss of her own.

My mom walked through the door, strangely composed, though she looked like she'd aged a decade.

Ryan, Sofia and I all stood to meet her, and it was Ryan who was the first to hug her, then Sofia, then me. I knew my mom would probably just like to go home, but I didn't want her to be alone. "Mom," I said gently. "How about you stay with me tonight? You can have Ryan's room. I don't think you should be alone tonight."

Her bottom lip trembled, and all she did was nod. She didn't want to leave Dad; she didn't want to go home without him. I understood that, and I was helpless to do anything about it.

I put my arm around her and led her out to my car. The drive to the city, to my place, was quiet, the both of us lost in our own thoughts. Through all of this, with my grieving mother in the seat next to me, all I could think about was Cooper.

I needed him.

I felt selfish for wanting him. I wanted to call him, I wanted to talk to him, I wanted to hear his voice. I just needed him.

But I couldn't.

He couldn't do anything by being here. He just had one day away for work, and he'd be back tomorrow.

I could hold out until then.

I got Mom inside my apartment, and Ryan and Sofia followed us in. Mom didn't want anyone to fuss. She didn't want to eat. She didn't want anything.

Just my dad.

I'd never felt more helpless.

Everyone was hurting and I couldn't do anything. I ordered food that no one ate; I only seemed to say the wrong thing, or not enough, or too much.

Mom said the doctor had given her a few pills to help her sleep tonight. I couldn't protest. I couldn't tell her she hadn't eaten all day. I couldn't say anything. I just gave her a hug, tucked her into bed and told her we'd deal with tomorrow together.

When I walked back into the kitchen, Sofia and Ryan both stood up and looked at me. "How is she?" Ryan asked.

"I think she's in shock," I told them. "Dad was fine at breakfast, and now he's gone. That has to be hard for anyone."

Ryan walked over to me. "You okay, Dad?"

No. No, I wasn't. "Yeah, I'm okay." I looked at both Ryan and Sofia. "You don't have to stay..." I was fighting to keep it together, swallowing back tears.

Then Sofia, who had been relatively quiet the entire day, came over to me and put her arms around me. It was kind and familiar, and it should have comforted me.

But it felt wrong.

She was soft and gentle, smelled floral and womanly, when all I wanted was firm and hard and the smell of cologne.

I pulled out of her embrace and took a step away. I swallowed hard and took a shaky breath.

"Tom, do you want us to stay?" she asked, looking a little concerned.

"No," I answered, trying not to cry. "I mean, you can if you want, but I'll be fine."

I didn't want to be rude. Sofia had been very gracious today, very kind and supportive. But she wasn't who I needed.

I walked around my ex-wife toward the sofa when there was a familiar sound of jingling keys in the lock of the front door.

I looked at Ryan.

"I called him," he said. "For you."

I turned back to the door as Cooper walked in. He looked worried, urgent, like he'd run all the way from Philly. He didn't look at anyone else. He put his bag on the floor and never took his eyes off me.

I'd never needed someone so fucking much.

There was a burning in my eyes and a heavy relief in my chest. I couldn't fight the tears, and a quiet sob escaped me.

Cooper crossed the floor and pulled me against him. He wrapped his arms around me, and I buried my face in his neck. He had one hand around my back and the other holding my head, and I'd never held anyone so tight. My hands fisted the back of his suit jacket, and he held me while I cried.

He fit against me perfectly. He felt right—his arms, his smell. Everything. He was... everything.

I didn't want to let go but eventually pulled back and wiped at my face. "I'm sorry you had to leave work. I'm sorry you had to come back," I said quietly. "But I'm so glad you're here."

Cooper nodded and wiped my face with his hands. "Tom, I'm so sorry."

"Thank you for coming," I whispered.

He held my face and kissed my cheek, then my forehead. He replied softly in my ear, "I couldn't be anywhere else."

I looked around then, at Ryan and Sofia, who were looking at Cooper and me. Cooper looked at Ryan and didn't hesitate. He took a few quick strides to him and hugged him too. "Thank you for calling me," he told him. "I'm really sorry, Ry."

Ryan hugged him back, and Cooper looked at Sofia. He walked slowly over to her. "Mrs. Elkin," he said gently. "I'm very sorry for your loss."

Sofia gave him a small, kind, but genuine smile. "Thank you, Cooper."

Then Cooper came back to me. He slid one hand around my jaw and gave me a quick kiss on the cheek. He wiped my face dry with his thumbs. "Have you eaten? Can I pour you a glass of wine? A coffee?"

I smiled, despite my tears, and put my hand on his chest. "I'm so glad you're here."

Cooper took my hand and led me to the sofa. "You guys sit down. I'm sure you have a lot of things to discuss," he said to us. "I'll make some hot tea."

He just took charge. He tidied up, put the leftover,

uneaten dinner in the fridge and came back with a tray of herbal tea and cups. "When my grandma died," he explained softly, "my mom served a lot of chamomile and peppermint tea. It's supposed to be calming and good for the soul." He sat down next to me and started to pour some of the hot brew into one of the four cups, then he stopped and looked up. "I think that's the gayest thing I've ever said."

Ryan snorted out a laugh, which made me chuckle. Even Sofia smiled. It was a much-needed release from the tears and the grief.

Cooper finished pouring the tea and I told him my mom was asleep in the spare room. We weren't sure what tomorrow would bring, but we'd deal with it the best we could.

He sat particularly close to me, with one leg tucked up underneath him, a part of him always touching me. Just having him there was a relief, like I could somehow bear the loss of my father if Cooper was with me.

The weight of the day, the irreparable loss, finally settled over me. I was suddenly exhausted and could barely keep my eyes open. When I stifled a yawn, Cooper suggested I go to bed.

He gave my leg a squeeze, got up from the sofa, then cleared away the tray and the tea. Cooper disappeared down the hall, came back with linens, and kicked us off the sofa so Ryan and Sofia would have somewhere to sleep. His insistence seemed to have surprised Sofia, but Ryan and I weren't surprised at all.

I offered to help, but he shooed me away. "You go in and have a hot shower," he said gently. "It will make you feel better. I'll get this all straightened out."

I loved his ability to just take charge, to know I needed

someone to take care of things, to take care of me. And he just did it. He just knew.

I stood under the stream of the hot water, and the realization that I'd lost my father hit me again. My own mortality hit me. How quickly life could change, how it could be changed forever in a heartbeat. I worried about my mother, how she would cope, how she would get through this.

Selfishly, I wondered how my life would change after today. Would my mom need to live with me? What would that mean for me and Cooper?

I shut off the water, and as I dressed in sleep pants and a T-shirt, I could hear someone was in the other shower in the main bathroom. Then I could hear two voices coming from the living room.

Soft voices, and at first I assumed it was Cooper and Ryan. But as I slipped into the hallway, I realized it was Cooper and Sofia. I knew I shouldn't have been listening. It was a private conversation. But it sounded amicable, so I stood there, where they couldn't see me, and listened.

"Did he really ask you to move in with him?" Sofia asked.

"Yes," Cooper answered honestly. "Several times."

"Why did you say no?"

Cooper laughed. "I like to keep him on his toes."

"But you want to move in with him?" Sofia asked.

I thought about moving, walking out so they'd hear me. I wasn't sure I wanted to hear his answer. I didn't think I could cope with hearing why. But then he spoke.

"Of course I do," he said quietly. "I love him."

My heart swelled in my chest at his words; my eyes filled with tears as I smiled.

"You know," Sofia started, "I've known Tom for a long

time. Since we were kids ourselves. We've been through a lot. I've been with him through everything—the highs and lows of his career, parenthood..."

I wondered where she was going with this, and I almost interrupted them.

But then she let out a nervous breath. "But tonight, when you walked into this apartment, when he saw you... the way he looked at you..." She paused for a moment and her voice was quiet. "In all the years we were together, not once did he ever look at me like that."

"Sofia..." Cooper started to speak.

"It's okay, Cooper," she said. "Really, it is. In a way, I'm glad."

"Glad?"

Sofia sighed again. "When I first learned that he and you were... Well, I thought it was just some fling. I thought it was something he'd get over," she admitted. "But I can see now that it's not."

"No, it's not," he replied. His tone was soft and agreeable.

"So I'm glad," she repeated. "I'm glad he has you."

The water from Ryan's shower cut off, and so I wasn't caught eavesdropping in the hallway, I had to move. I walked out into the living room. Cooper and Sofia were sitting at the dining table, and he stood up when I walked in. "Feel a bit better?"

I smiled at him. "Yeah, but I should go to bed. No doubt Mom will be up with the sun in the morning." Sliding my hand along Cooper's arm, I gave him a soft kiss.

"I won't be long," he whispered.

I mouthed the words "I love you" so only he could see, then I kissed Sofia on the forehead. "Thank you for being here," I told her. And I meant it.

I said a quiet goodnight to Ryan as he walked out, gave him a hug, and I climbed into bed. As exhausted as I was, as emotionally drained as I was, I closed my eyes, but sleep wouldn't come. Soon after, familiar, strong arms wrapped around me and I turned to face him. It was only when Cooper tucked me into his side and kissed my forehead, that I fell into sleep.

CHAPTER THIRTEEN

I WOKE up and smiled at Cooper's sleeping form beside me. Then I remembered the events of yesterday—that my father had died.

My stomach knotted and my heart sank.

Then I remembered my mother was asleep in the room across the hall.

It was still early, so I threw on some jeans and a shirt and set about making breakfast.

Cooper, sleep-rumpled and gorgeous, woke up to the scent of coffee. Ryan woke up to the smell of toast. Sofia smiled at the both of them playfully bickering over who would eat first as she folded up the sheets from the sofas in the living room.

I worried Cooper might find it weird that he was having breakfast with my son and my ex-wife, but he seemed to take it all in stride. He took over the kitchen like he owned it, finishing up cooking and cleaning.

But then my mother walked out to where we were. She looked like hell. Her eyes were red and puffy, she was pale and... heartbroken.

I walked over to her and gave her a hug. "Coffee?" I asked, and she nodded.

She sat down on the sofa, and when I glanced over at Cooper, he seemed nervous. He grabbed a coffee cup, and before he could pour it, Sofia was beside him. "Go," she murmured.

It was then that my mother looked at who else was there. Her eyes landed on Cooper.

I cleared my throat. "Ah, Mom?" I said, and she looked at me. "I want you to meet someone."

Cooper's eyes darted to mine, but he walked around the kitchen island, nervously wiping the palms of his hands on his thighs.

I took Cooper's hand and we sat down across from my mother. "Mom, this is Cooper Jones," I said. I figured there was no easy way to say this, and there was no point in beating around the bush. "Cooper and I are together, Mom. We're dating."

My mother blinked. And then blinked again.

"I'm gay, Mom," I told her. "I know the timing is horrible. I know you're dealing with a lot right now, but in light of yesterday... with Dad... I don't want to wait another day. I don't want to keep any secrets from you."

Mom was silent, unmoving.

"I'm in love with Cooper," I added gently. "And life's too damn short, Mom."

Cooper squeezed my hand, just as Sofia brought over a cup of coffee and handed it to Mom. Then Sofia sat down next to my mother and squeezed her hand.

Mom looked at her. "You know about this?"

"I do," Sofia said with a gentle smile. "It's okay. I didn't take it well at first, I'll admit to that. But yesterday, well, yesterday I saw them in a different light."

Mom looked at Cooper then, studied him for a long moment, then looked at me. "A boy?"

"Not a boy," I corrected softly. "A man. And yes."

Mom put her coffee down on the side table untouched. "You're telling me this today?"

"Today especially," I said softly. My eyes burned with unshed tears. I didn't want this to turn sour. I knew the timing was awful, but I had to tell her. She had to know. "Today especially, Mom. After yesterday... losing Dad... Mom, if there was ever a day to tell you how much I loved someone, then today is it."

Mom's lip trembled, and she blinked back tears. Deciding to ignore my point of conversation altogether, she picked up her coffee again with shaking hands and said, "I need to call the hospital, I guess. I need to make a lot of calls and tell people..."

"Mom, I can phone them," I offered. "Just tell me who you want me to call."

Then Mom started to talk about letting the Country Club know and an aunt who lived on the West Coast, and how Julia, her next-door neighbor, must be worried sick.

"I'll take you home if you want," I said softly.

"Would you, dear?" she said. "I have a lot to do." Then her eyes welled with tears. "I'm not sure how I'll do it without him..."

Ryan walked around then and hugged his grandma. "We're here to help you," he said. "All of us." I couldn't help but smile at Ryan's inclusion of Cooper, and I squeezed Cooper's hand.

"I'll just go freshen up first," Mom said before she stood, leaving us all in the living room, and walked down the hall.

Cooper ran his hand up my back and into my hair, and he pulled me against him. "I'm sorry," I murmured to him.

He kissed the side of my head and whispered, "Don't apologize."

Sofia stood up. "I can take her home, if you'd like, Tom."

For a moment, I considered it. "I'll take her," I said. "But thank you for the offer." I looked at Cooper. "I just wish I didn't have to leave you."

"You need to go," he said with serious eyes. "You need to be with your mom."

As much as I needed to be with Cooper, I needed to be with my Mom more. "What will you do?"

"He'll come home with me," Ryan interrupted. "I have a new Xbox 3D that needs playing," he went on to say. Then he shrugged. "And I could use the company."

Cooper smiled and looked at Ryan, Sofia then me. "Don't worry about me, silly. You go, take care of your mom."

Everyone knew I was worried about how I'd be without him, not the other way around, but no one acknowledged it out loud. Five minutes later, I kissed Cooper soundly, told them I'd call each of them, and took my mother home.

We spent the day making phone calls and making arrangements. It was emotionally draining, and by the time Mom put herself to bed, I didn't want to leave her in the house alone.

I called Ryan, then Sofia, like I said I would, then I called Cooper. I spoke in a whisper, not wanting to wake my mother, but desperately needing to hear his voice.

I told him I wouldn't be back for another night at least, that I'd call the office in the morning and request a week's leave. "They're hoping to have the funeral on Thursday," I said. "Do you think you could come with me?"

"Oh, Tom," he whispered into the phone. "Of course I'll be there."

I sighed, almost with relief, knowing he'd be with me. "I miss you," I said rather pathetically.

"Babe, I'm just a phone call away," he replied. "But if you need me to come, I'll leave right now."

I smiled sadly into the phone. "Just hearing your voice is enough. But thank you."

"You sound tired," he said softly. "Don't hang up. Go to bed, and we can talk again when you're ready for sleep."

I walked into the guest bedroom, and leaving my jeans on the floor, I climbed into bed, and we talked. Quietly, tenderly, without any physical contact, we spoke for hours. Cooper knew I needed him on some level, like he always just knew.

I loved him, this man who was half my age and twice as strong as me.

I'd never loved him more.

THE NEXT MORNING, I called work and spoke to Robert Chandler and explained I needed some time off. He sent warm, honest condolences and told me to take as much time as I needed. Then I spent the rest of the day at the hospital, and it was that night it really hit my mom that my dad was gone.

She cried and cried and spent the entire evening wandering around the house, trying to keep busy. She had phone call after phone call of people with good intentions, but in the end I started answering the phone for her.

It was a restless night, but Tuesday was marginally better. I spent the entire time with her, rarely leaving her side, yet she never once mentioned my little coming out speech, and she never mentioned Cooper.

It wasn't surprising. It was typical of my mother to ignore subjects she didn't want to discuss. I did mention Cooper in conversation a few times, but she never asked me anything. It was hardly the time to bring it up. She knew I was gay, she knew I was in love with someone special, and that was all I wanted.

By Tuesday evening, I couldn't put it off any longer. I needed to go home, back to New York. I needed to get clothes for the funeral, so Mom's neighbor Julia kindly offered to stay with her. I drove straight back to the city and didn't even bother going home.

I drove straight to Cooper's.

He opened the door to his shoebox apartment, and the second he saw me, he pulled me into his arms.

He was like fucking oxygen to drowning lungs.

He took me straight to bed, holding me so damn tight as he made love to me. He kissed me so reverently; he wiped my tears and his eyes never left mine as he rocked his hips into mine. He filled me so completely—physically, emotionally.

He just knew. He knew exactly what I needed, and he gave it to me without question.

I woke with my face to his chest and his long fingers tracing circles on my back. He had to go to work, and I had to go back to Mom's. But with a soft kiss and a whispered 'I love you,' we went our separate ways.

I was kept busy with final funeral arrangements and organizing the wake. I spoke to Cooper briefly on the phone Wednesday night, and by the time we were ready for the funeral on Thursday, I was just about ready to unravel.

Mom wanted to get to the church early. She wanted to be there to greet the good people as they came in. All things considered, she was coping quite well. It was the first time in two days that I'd had time to stop, and standing alone beside a flower-covered casket didn't help.

I said somber hellos and thanks to the people who came in. Lots of faces I recognized, lots I didn't. Most surprising was two very familiar faces from work—Jennifer and Robert had wanted to show their support in being there for me. I'd worked with them for a decade, and I was touched very deeply by their presence.

Then Sofia walked in, looking lovely and impeccably dressed, and she gave me a sad smile. Behind her was Ryan, all suited up, then behind him was Cooper.

Wearing a black suit, his hair styled and clean-shaven, he walked into the fast-filling church and he visibly sighed when he saw me. I can't begin to describe the relief I felt when I saw him. It rocked me. I took a steadying breath and blinked back tears.

Sofia gave me a soft pat on the arm and took a seat at the end of the front row. Ryan gave me a hug and took his seat next to his mother, then Cooper was standing in front of me.

I didn't care that people were watching. I didn't care what they thought. I hugged him, and I hugged him hard. It wasn't a family-friend hug; it wasn't a thanks-for-coming hug. It was an embrace.

Cooper pulled back and whispered, "You'll be okay."

"I will now," I told him.

Cooper took a seat next to Ryan, and when my mom came in, I put my arm around her and led her to the front row. I sat next to Cooper and took his hand immediately and slid my other arm around my mom as the funeral started.

The priest talked of a well-loved man, whose life was cut far too short. He spoke of family, loss, and of acceptance and love, and when he said I'd be getting up to talk to the congregation, I didn't hear him call my name.

"Tom?" Cooper said quietly beside me. "Did you want to get up and talk?"

"Oh," I said, apparently a million miles away.

"You don't have to," he said, concerned. "Everyone will understand."

"No, I'm okay," I told him, then I stood up and walked up to the lectern. I ran the prepared notes through my head, and when I looked at the faces staring back at me, all the words in my head were gone.

I glanced over at the priest and exhaled through puffed cheeks. "I, um," I started. "When I was asked if I'd like to say something in honor of my father, I said I would. Of course I would." I swallowed hard. "But what I was going to say doesn't seem fitting.

"My father was a good man. A good father, a good husband, and a good friend," I told them. "My father was one of the biggest influences in my life. He hated architecture," I said, and a few people smiled. "He told me I should get into banking or teaching, but I followed my heart. And it was his initial disapproval that pushed me to be the best. I didn't want to disappoint him."

My gaze fell on Cooper then, and I swallowed back my tears. If only my father knew how much I would have disappointed him...

I shook my head and took a deep breath so I could keep talking. "But funnily enough, my dad and architecture were a lot alike. And whether he knew it or not, he taught me more about architecture than college ever could."

I looked at my mother, then at Ryan and Sofia. "He taught me that solid foundations gave me strength and stability. He taught me that the only principles of design should be honesty and integrity, and above all, that there was a truth in the lines that we drew."

Finally I looked back at Cooper and had to blink back tears. "It's unfortunate that some of life's greatest lessons come from death. Because without knowing it, my father taught me that *every* design has a clarity of lines. Lines that bind it, that define it, that make it—lines that sometimes other people can't see." I scanned the faces around the church then, not ashamed of my tears. "And that's what I'll take with me—what my father taught me. That sometimes the lines seemed undefined, but they aren't blurred at all. Sometimes they're crystal clear."

I thanked everyone for coming, to help celebrate the life of a good man, then I walked back to my seat and slid my arm around my crying mother. Cooper took my hand and held it tight, and for the rest of the service, he never let it go.

Throughout the wake, Cooper was never far away. I didn't care if distant relatives, work colleagues, or complete strangers saw me with my arm around his waist or if they saw the way I looked at him.

Life was too damn short.

We'd done the rounds of talking and thanking the guests, and after many stories of my father's life, the crowd eventually waned. Mom had tired quickly, and when I had suggested I take her home and stay with her, Sofia put her hand on my arm. "I'll take her. I'll spend the night with her. You should go," she said with a kind smile.

"Are you sure?"

"Of course I'm sure," she said. "You look tired, Tom. Let Cooper take you home."

I hugged her, taking her off guard, and I thanked her. Her final acceptance of Cooper in my life meant the world to me.

Then Cooper hugged her as well. "Thank you, Sofia," he said softly.

We said goodbye to Ryan, and Cooper took my keys and told me he was driving. I didn't even argue. Instead, I half turned in my seat so I faced him and watched him while he drove. He held my hand over the console, and after a little while, he told me he'd had a few talks with Sofia these last few days.

He told me of the conversation I'd half over-heard, about how she could see now that we were the real deal. She admitted to him the age difference between us had worried her, but she knew now it didn't matter.

"Plus, she thinks I'm charming and handsome and awesome," Cooper said.

"She did not say that," I said tiredly.

"I'm paraphrasing," he said.

Leaning my head against the headrest, not taking my eyes off him, I smiled. "God, I've missed you."

Cooper smiled and squeezed my hand. "We're almost home. Do you want dinner? A bath? Alcohol?"

I shook my head. "Nothing. I just want to be with you."

He pulled the car into the parking lot, then took the elevator straight to our floor. He threw the keys to my car onto the kitchen counter and led me down the hall to my bedroom.

He took off his jacket then helped me out of mine. "Does it feel good to be home?"

"It does. It's weird though," I admitted.

Cooper undid his shirt. "What's weird?"

"I'm the next in line now. Genealogically speaking, father-to-son, I should be the next one to go."

Cooper shook his head. "No. Don't say that."

"Not now," I amended. "Just... next. Now that my dad's gone, like his father before him and his before that."

Cooper frowned and he started to undo the buttons on my shirt. "I called my dad," he said. "After... When you took your mom back to her house and after Ry and Sofia left and I was alone here, I called him."

"Really?"

He nodded. "I didn't want to leave things bad between us. I mean, the last time we spoke wasn't exactly on the best terms." His brow pinched. "I told him about your dad... I told him I didn't want that to be us. I'm sorry if that sounds bad..."

"I understand, Cooper," I told him honestly. "And he was okay?"

Cooper nodded and gave me a small smile. "Better. He was better."

I slid my hand around his neck and pulled him in for a kiss. "That's great."

He smiled and went to put my pants and jacket on a hanger but felt the folded paper in my breast pocket. "What's this?" he asked as he passed the handwritten notes to me.

"It's the speech I was going to say at the funeral," I said with a shrug. "Instead, I just... spoke from the heart. What I said at the funeral probably didn't make much sense."

Cooper stopped undressing and put his hand to my face. "What you said in the church made a lot of sense," he murmured. "It was beautiful."

I nodded, then undressed down to my briefs, pulled back the bedcovers, and got into bed. Cooper quickly joined me, lying on his side, facing me.

I took his hand and played with his fingers. "These last few months, people have judged us, told us that us being together is wrong, just because I'm twice your age, or if they think it's just some fling," I told him. "I wanted to tell people that the lines aren't blurred for me. I know exactly what I want. And having my father taken away so suddenly was like a wake-up call for me."

"Your speech was lovely," he said simply, threading his fingers through mine. Then after a quiet moment, he asked, "What were you going to say? What was written on the piece of paper?"

"It was just some childhood memories of my father." I sighed. "It was nice to relive those memories, but no one really wants to hear those kinds of stories at funerals. They mean a lot to me, but not to anyone else."

"Tell me," Cooper said softly. "Tell me your childhood memories, like what was your favorite memory of your dad when you were little."

I leaned in and kissed him lightly. "You're amazing, you know that?"

"Yes, I do," he said with a smile. "It's a Cooper-Jones thing, remember?"

"How could I forget?" I said, and for the next little while, until I couldn't fight sleep any longer, I relived childhood memories of a boy and his father.

———

TWO WEEKS LATER, it was a Saturday and I was drawing at the drafting board in the living room. Cooper said he had some errands to run in the morning but had arrived not long after lunch and threw himself onto the sofa.

He was agitated, which was very un-Cooper-like. "You know, you haven't asked me to live with you for a while."

I smiled at the board. "I got sick of hearing no."

He tapped his fingers on the arm of the chair. "I kept saying no because you kept asking me wrong. Did you want to try it again?"

"Is your lease terminating?" I asked with a smile, putting my graphite pencil down. "Is that why you want to move in with me? Is this some Gen Y, the-world-revolves-around-me thing?"

He sighed dramatically. "Oh, Tom. You're getting the move-in-with-me speech wrong *again*."

I laughed at him, but realizing he was finally asking me to do this, I quickly walked over and knelt between his legs. I looked up at him. "Move in with me, Cooper. I want to go to sleep with you. I want to wake up next to you. Every day. I want to live with you. I want to know everything about you. I want you to show me how you see the world." Then I added, "I want to show you things like the different architecture all around the world, all the amazing places. I want to share *that* with you. You are perfect for me, Cooper." I sat back on my haunches and shrugged. "You've changed me, and I don't want to live without you."

He smiled slowly.

"Did I get it right that time?"

He nodded. "And just so you know, I have a month left on the lease on my apartment, but I've given notice. I'm completely packed and ready to move in."

Grinning, I leaned up and pecked his lips. "A little confident that I'd still want you to live with me, yes?"

He closed his eyes and smiled. "It's a Gen-Y thing."

"It's a Cooper-Jones thing."

"No, it's an I-love-you thing."

"It's an I-love-you-too thing."

"So are we doing the whole-live-in-boyfriend thing?"

"Yes."

He grinned. "Lionel will be so stoked."

"Are you moving in here because you have a crush on the doorman?"

"No, no," he said, like I'd missed the point. "He has a crush on me."

"You're incorrigible."

Cooper leaned forward and kissed me with smiling lips. "You really shouldn't talk about your live-in boyfriend like that."

I sighed. "There really is no point in arguing, is there?"

He shook his head. "No. But Tom?"

"Yeah?"

"Don't ever stop arguing with me."

"I won't."

"Promise?"

"Promise."

EPILOGUE

Cooper

MY CELL PHONE RANG. It was my dad's number. My heart leaped and sank at the same time. I'd called him after Tom's father had died, telling him perspective put a new light on things, and he'd seemed to agree. I refused to apologize for falling in love—not that he asked me to apologize—but it was really only time that would tell if he was truly okay with Tom and me. And that's why I was nervous.

"Hey," I answered.

"Hiya." He sounded upbeat. "How are things?"

"Good, good."

"Settling into domestic life okay?"

I snorted. "Just fine. How're things with you?"

He launched into telling me about some dinner Mom was making him go to, and he wanted some tips on any serious illness he could fake to get out of going. So in between suggestions of chest pains, spider bites, and actually growing a set of cojones, we were back to good. Just like old times. I sat my ass on the sofa, put my bare feet on the coffee table, and laughed with my dad.

It was such a relief, such a weight off my chest, that even after we'd said our goodbyes and disconnected the call, I sat there and smiled at the wall for a while. I couldn't wait to tell Tom.

Eventually I got up and padded around the apartment. Well, it was Tom's apartment, which I now called home. I'd officially lived there a week. Just seven days. My things—the few things that I owned—were here, looking all sorts of cheap and tacky compared to Tom's expensive and classical taste. The differences stood out ridiculously.

But Tom refused to hide them. "They remind me that you live here," he'd said. Then he'd looked around our bedroom at all my clothes and shit on the floor. "Not that I could ever forget."

But he was serious. He wanted my things here on display as much as his own, and the truth was Tom didn't see my belongings as inferior in any way. They belonged to me, and that was enough for him to want to show them off proudly.

And people wondered why I loved him?

I picked up my dirty socks and threw them in the clothes hamper. I really had to make more of an effort now. Be more grown up, I supposed. Tom might think my clothes strewn across the bedroom was cute now, but there would no doubt be a time when it would piss him off, and I just didn't want that day to come.

So I tidied up everything, then collected my suits and shirts ready for dry cleaning, then seeing Tom's, I added his to mine and called for a service collection. I didn't go as far as cleaning the bathrooms or anything. I didn't have to. Tom had cleaners for that.

Such luxury would never get old.

Nothing in this apartment would ever cease to blow my mind. Tom included.

He was with Ryan and Sofia, having lunch downtown. He'd asked me to join them, of course, but I wanted him to have some alone time with them. Especially with the death of his father just over two weeks ago, they needed to decompress and take some time to be together, just the three of them.

Tom had kissed me and whispered, "Thank you." Whether he was thanking me for understanding, or thanking me for just being fucking awesome, I wasn't sure. It could have very well been both.

I'd just pulled his chin between my thumb and forefinger and kissed his lips. "Be home at two, and be alone," I'd told him. My voice had been gruff and dripping with sexual promise.

I couldn't help it. I was a twenty-two-year-old gay guy living with the sexiest man on the fucking planet. I was horny all the damn time. It was Tom's fault completely. He stimulated my mind and my body equally.

My boss, Louisa, benefited from the former; Tom from the latter. Not that he minded. Hell, he didn't mind at all.

My plan was for him to come home and find me, stark naked and ass up on the bed, ready and waiting. I wanted him to fuck me for hours, and when he was done fucking me, he could damn well fuck me some more.

But I lost track of time. It was the first time I'd really been in the apartment by myself for any great length, and somewhere between spending an hour on the balcony overlooking my kingdom—which some folk liked to call New York City—and going through Tom's wardrobe seeing which of his suits might fit me, time just got away from me.

I'd barely got myself douched in the bathroom before I heard his key in the front door.

Shit, shit, shit.

I quickly pulled on my jeans and went out to see him. He stopped when he saw me, his eyes were dark and focused, and he looked a little peeved.

"Hey. What's up?" I asked.

He put his keys on the table as he walked in. "Be home by two." He repeated my earlier demand, striding over to me. "Be alone." He walked around me and sniffed me.

Was he smelling the douche? Jesus. My dick stirred.

He huffed his disapproval. His voice was deep and low when he whispered, "Your promise had me distracted all lunch and I come home to find you not naked."

Oh, wow. That demanding tone in his voice buzzed straight to my cock. "I ran out of time," I offered meekly, playing along. I went to undo my fly, but he stopped me.

"Leave them on."

I did as I'd been told, trying not to smile.

He stood in front of me, put a finger under my chin so I looked up at him. His eyes were on fire, making me swallow hard, then he almost—almost—pressed his lips to mine. But he didn't. He teased, taunted, instead of touched, and withholding the kiss I craved, he said, "Go stand at the drafting table."

Oh, holy fuck.

Now, I'd never let anyone boss me around, but this... this was different. *This* was about to be a whole lotta fun.

I walked slowly over to the drafting board and stood facing it, hands by my sides. I could feel his eyes on me, every hair on the back of my neck was on end, my dick was hard and my skin flushed warm with a promise of what was to come.

He waited a long moment, and I wondered if he was about to laugh and this game would be over, but he didn't. I turned to find him walking from the hall with a silver foil packet and lube in his hand.

"Turn around," he demanded.

I quickly did as he'd said. My skin prickled with gooseflesh and my nipples hardened. I widened my stance and rolled my hips so my ass stuck out more. Fuck. This was too good.

He stood behind me, close enough that I could feel the warmth of his body, but he didn't touch me.

"Grip the top of the board," he said, all gruff like sex and honey.

Every cell in my body caught fire at his words. He knew this was a fantasy of mine—I'd told him it was. We'd had sex against the drafting board before, but my fantasy wasn't just having sex. It was him taking me, dominating me, fucking me so damn hard... And holy Jesus, he was making it happen. Aching in all the right places, I bit back a moan. I reached up over my head and gripped the top of the drafting board.

He pressed himself against me then. "Keep your hands up there." He reached around to my front and undid my jeans, deliberately brushing against my hard-on, then he roughly pulled the denim down over my ass.

"Fuck," I whispered, and I could feel my blood pump hot through my whole body. I was so turned on.

Tom put his legs between mine and shoved my feet out wider still. My jeans were tight across my thighs, my ass exposed, and I let my head fall forward with a moan.

Like every sense was on keen alert, I heard the pop of the lube bottle, and the sound made my skin tingle. Then his slick fingers were rubbing over my hole and pushing inside me. I cried out, not because he was rough or hurt me, but because it wasn't enough. It was torture. The very best kind of torture.

"I know what you want," he murmured in my ear, sliding in a second finger. I lifted my ass to give him more access. It felt so good, so very fucking good, but it still wasn't enough—and he knew it.

Then his fingers were gone and I heard him undo his fly, and I almost came right then. He never took his boots off, so I knew his jeans were still on, only opened at the fly. I heard the foil packet rip open, and my body instinctively pushed my ass out. God, I wanted him inside me like I never had before.

He pressed the head of his blunt cock against my ass and his breath was hot in my ear. "This what you want?"

All I could do was nod.

And he thrust inside me. Hard and deep, he grunted and groaned, and his hands gripped my hips as he buried every inch of his cock in me. Then his hands, his oh-so-talented hands, raked roughly up my sides, up my outstretched arms and held my hands over the drafting board.

"Fuck," he cried out, gruff and hot, as he started to thrust.

He wasn't gentle. He fucked me. He fucked me like I wanted him to, needed him to. I was so stretched and full, my arms reaching out above my head, and my toes barely on the floor as he drove up and into me, over and over.

I tried to pull my hand down so I could grip my aching dick, but he forcefully grabbed both my hands and held them in one of his at the edge of the drafting board. He took hold of my cock in his now-free hand and jerked me hard and fast as he filled my ass.

I wanted to tell him to never stop, to keep doing exactly fucking that, but I couldn't even speak. All I could do was groan as I came. My orgasm obliterated my insides, pleasure so intense and hot barreled through me, and he never stopped fucking. I let my head fall back against his shoulder, my body completely at his will—he owned me. I was his. I never had any doubt.

He grunted in my ear, words I couldn't understand, and he roared as he climaxed. His cock surged and swelled inside me, and I could feel his knees and thighs shake before he leaned against me, spent. Exhausted.

I felt him grin against my back before groaning as he pulled out of me. I turned around as he threw the condom in the trash, and ignoring the wonderful ache in my ass, I cupped his face and kissed him. When I wrapped my arms around him, he kind of fell into me, pressing my back against the drafting board.

He was all slow and languid, his eyes barely open. He had a blissed-out look on his face. "You okay?" he asked, his voice husky and low.

I snorted and held him tighter. "I'm so fucking better than okay right now."

I pushed him back a little so I could grab his hand. I led him down the hall to our room, my jeans still around my thighs, his softening dick still heavy and glistening, hanging free, and I pulled him onto the bed and snuggled into him.

"I'm still dressed," he mumbled. "Should probably shower."

"Mm-hmm," I protested, holding him right where was. "Nap first. You can fuck me again later."

He snorted, his eyes still closed and relaxed. "Haven't you had enough?"

"Never."

"You're insatiable."

"Can't help it," I said, drowsily. "My live-in boyfriend is really fucking hot."

He smiled against my forehead. "Is he?"

"Yeah, and I want to spend the rest of the day with his dick in my ass."

Tom opened his eyes at that. They took a second to focus. "Is that right?"

"Yep."

"Do you always get what you want?"

I grinned, closed my eyes, and snuggled in warm against him. "You've met me, right?"

He laughed, a deep rumbling sound in my ear. "It's that damn Gen-Y thing."

I snuggled in some more and sighed, more content than I'd ever been. "It's a Cooper-Jones thing."

Tom took a deep breath and tightened his arms around me. He pressed his lips to my forehead. "It's an I-love-you thing."

"Just as well," I mumbled sleepily. "I'd hate to think I moved in with just anyone."

He sighed and gave me a gentle squeeze but never said anything more.

"Tom?"

"Yes?"

"I love you, too."

The End

CLARITY OF LINES

N.R. WALKER

THE THOMAS ELKIN SERIES

Book One: Elements of Retrofit
Book Two: Clarity of Lines
Book Three: Sense of Place

ABOUT THE AUTHOR

N.R. Walker is an Australian author, who loves her genre of gay romance. She loves writing and spends far too much time doing it, but wouldn't have it any other way.

She is many things: a mother, a wife, a sister, a writer. She has pretty, pretty boys who live in her head, who don't let her sleep at night unless she gives them life with words.

She likes it when they do dirty, dirty things... but likes it even more when they fall in love.

She used to think having people in her head talking to her was weird, until one day she happened across other writers who told her it was normal.

She's been writing ever since...

CONTACT THE AUTHOR
www.nrwalker.net
nrwalker@nrwalker.net

ALSO BY N.R. WALKER

The Spencer Cohen Series, Book Two

The Spencer Cohen Series, Book Three

The Spencer Cohen Series, Yanni's Story

Blood & Milk

The Weight Of It All

Perfect Catch

Switched

Imago

Imagines

Red Dirt Heart Imago

On Davis Row

Titles in Audio:

Cronin's Key

Cronin's Key II

Cronin's Key III

Red Dirt Heart

Red Dirt Heart 2

Red Dirt Heart 3

The Weight Of It All

Switched

Free Reads:

Sixty Five Hours

Learning to Feel

His Grandfather's Watch (And The Story of Billy and Hale)

The Twelfth of Never (Blind Faith 3.5)

Twelve Days of Christmas (Sixty Five Hours Christmas)

Best of Both Worlds

Translated Titles:

Fiducia Cieca (Italian translation of Blind Faith)

Attraverso Questi Occhi (Italian translation of Through These Eyes)

Preso alla Sprovvista (Italian translation of Blindside)

Il giorno del Mai (Italian translation of Blind Faith 3.5)

Cuore di Terra Rossa (Italian translation of Red Dirt Heart)

Cuore di Terra Rossa 2 (Italian translation of Red Dirt Heart 2)

Cuore di Terra Rossa 3 (Italian translation of Red Dirt Heart 3)

Cuore di Terra Rossa 4 (Italian translation of Red Dirt Heart 4)

Confiance Aveugle (French translation of Blind Faith)

A travers ces yeux: Confiance Aveugle 2 (French translation of Through These Eyes)

Aveugle: Confiance Aveugle 3 (French translation of Blindside)

À Jamais (French translation of Blind Faith 3.5)

Cronin's Key (French translation)

Cronin's Key II (French translation)

Au Coeur de Sutton Station (French translation of Red Dirt Heart)

9 781925 886344